A SMALL COUNTRY ABOUT TO VANISH

Also by Victoria Avilan

The Art of Peeling an Orange

A Small Country about to Vanish

a novel

Victoria Avilan

Copyright © 2015 Victoria Avilan
All rights reserved.

Shaggy Dog Stories

Copyright © 2015 Victoria Avilan
Cover design by Victoria Avilan
Cover photo by an unknown artist
Author's photo on back cover by Suzanne Gross
Edited by Beth Hill

A Small Country about to Vanish : a novel / Victoria Avilan. — 1st edition.
ISBN-13: 978-1514349298 (paperback)
ISBN-10: 1514349299
ASIN: B00YFCRVF6 (eBook)

All rights reserved, including without limitation the right to reproduce this book or any portion thereof in any form or by any means, whether electronic or mechanical, now known or hereinafter invented, including photocopy, recording, or any information storage and retrieval system, without the written permission of the author.

This is a work of fiction. Names, characters, places, events, and incidents either are the product of the author's imagination or are used fictitiously. Any resemblance to actual persons, living or dead, businesses, companies, events, or locales is entirely coincidental.

Contact email : victoria@vicavilan.com
Author's website/blog : www.vicavilan.com
Visit Victoria Avilan's author page on facebook

Acknowledgements

For your mentoring through the UCLA Writers' Program and for words of wisdom that etched new grooves in my brain, I thank you, my dear friend and teacher, Claire Carmichael, Writing Guru Extraordinaire.

Editor Beth Hill, thank you for your brilliant insights and valuable advice.

Nili Sachs, thanks for occasionally attempting to restore my sanity.

My BFFs Patricia Gisler, Jeff and Suzie Gross, thank you for your constant help throughout the process. Special thanks to Teresa Bernau, Kathleen Harrigan-Hamamoto, and Kevin Amick.

Mocha, Indie and Max—for warming my feet when I write and for wagging when I don't.

My beloved wife Tracey Dodd, thank you for your encouragement, for letting me be, for being my first reader and editor and the reason for everything.

I thank my loving father Uzzi Levy, who gave me wings and showed me how to fly; and my mother, Miryam Levy, the first voracious reader I knew, who read books for me before I could read for myself and who taught me curiosity.

I love you all. You made writing and publishing this book possible and worth the effort.

For my beloved homeland

and all her people,

whose struggles are mine.

All opinions expressed in this novel are the opinions of fictional characters. If anyone or any group gets offended, please accept the author's apologies.

Part One
ISOLDE

A Small Country about to Vanish

1

"The Moonlight Sonata" envelops me again, and my mind follows its slow progression, returning me to a land so small and hungry, it devours its inhabitants, first sheltering them, then soaking in their blood. Devouring, yet growing ever smaller.

I lean against the balcony's railing in the relative serenity of my adopted country, listening and feeling. Remembering.

As the adagio streams like silvery molten lava from behind me and into the narrow alley, down Pier Avenue and into the breaking waves of the Pacific, I'm again a twelve-year-old dreamer, a girl fascinated by an ancient piano and with Rona Lubliner's fingers.

I was jealous of my friend Rona because her mother forced her to play the piano every afternoon from four to six. I could've been envious of her academic achievements, her popularity in school, or her sexy figure—none of which I had— but I envied her ability to play the piano.

Rona would have much preferred to hang out with her girlfriends, chase the boys and run as far as possible from her mother and her angry memories.

Eva—who had left Hungary for Israel before the Nazi rule, later losing her entire family in Buchenwald—would vigorously mop the floor with soapy water she'd saved from her morning bath. She'd use the rest of her bath water for the ficus, the philodendron and for various herbs she cultivated in rusted pots on the fourth floor balcony, one of many identical balconies, in a stained old apartment building in Tel Aviv.

I wanted to tell Eva how much I loved her piano and that she should stop wasting time on her ungrateful daughter and teach me instead. I would've made a better student because my social life was as good as dead anyway and, unlike Rona, I didn't give a shit about smelly boys. I wanted to tell her all those things, but Eva would have nothing to do with me.

As she scrubbed the floor, Eva would yell at her daughter in harsh Hungarian. Her Hebrew was too poor for real conversation. I don't know how well she spoke Hungarian, but she was loud. Her thick voice was old to my ears. She was only in her forties and already ancient with her swollen face, squarish body and coarse hair.

Rona would answer in Hebrew, "Ima, leave me alone!"

What a brat, I would think, sitting behind her on the brown couch with the paisley pattern, waiting for her to shut up and start playing.

Rona would eventually sit at the piano in spread-legged contempt, fling one of her long braids back and turn to glance at me, her eyes the shade of blue tinged with lavender, her lips white from being pressed tightly together.

"I'm so sick of her nagging," she'd blurt out, as if Eva wasn't there.

She'd start with the scales. Her practice was abrupt, and as rude as a spit in Eva's face, as brief as an afterthought and a masterpiece in itself. From scales she'd easily shift to Scriabin, Chopin or Beethoven.

"The Moonlight Sonata" affected me most because of the perfect harmony between its weighty, funereal *adagio sostenuto* and the Hungarian language. I couldn't understand Eva's words, but those heavenly sounds from the piano reverberated her immense losses and bottomless grief. I would listen in longing, letting Eva's scrubbing of the floor, that constant motion in my peripheral vision, become part of the experience.

It was an extraordinary piano—ebony black, upright with gold engravings, ivory keyboard, burgundy accents and silver candlesticks. Rona bragged that it was a hundred-year-old genuine Erard and that it had once been played by Franz Liszt. She wasn't sure, though. One day when we were alone, she unclipped the back of the piano and we shoved our heads into the darkness inside its soundboard. She aimed a flashlight on a long row of names.

"Look, Shelli." Her voice echoed in the dark. "All the tuners since 1872."

We searched, but we couldn't find Liszt's signature among the others.

Both Eva and I lived vicariously through Rona's playing. I would sometimes read a book, but mostly I'd drink in the sight and sounds of that old Erard and make-believe I was playing for a full house at Carnegie Hall. Or I'd fix my gaze on a framed sepia portrait on top of the piano, a photo of a woman, and wonder if she was another of Eva's losses.

The small room reeked of furniture polish and of the harsh soap Eva used for mopping.

While Rona played, Eva remained on her knees, sometimes scrubbing the same area on the spotless floor. Occasionally she'd pause midmop and glare up at her daughter's back with disapproval. Or she'd bark instructions: "*Staccato*." "*Legato*." "*Legatissimo*."

I was afraid of Eva's anger, of Rona's indignation. I couldn't understand any of it. What Rona could do was so wonderful. Such joy, being the channel for Beethoven, and all without looking at her hands even once.

"What's she yelling about?" I once asked. "What are chord and arpeggio fingerings?"

15

"This." Rona stuck up her middle finger in a rude gesture. "Something I hate because it buries me here two hours every day."

"I'd be happy to be buried this way," I said. Even if it meant someone yelling at me in an incomprehensible language. I dreamed of becoming a concert pianist, but according to Rona, piano lessons were out of the question for me.

"It's too late, Shelli." She chuckled. "As far as piano goes, your hands are considered arthritic. You have to start when you're three, when your fingers are supple and adaptable and your brain is a clean slate."

I knew my brain was all wrong, because it was turmoiled by thoughts and wishes. My fingers seemed normal, like those of any girl my age. But Rona's words were sacred, and so I didn't see the point of asking my parents for piano lessons.

If wishes were horses, whatever that proverb meant, there was Rona, riding my beloved horse because I could not, kicking it and denying it water. What a waste it was, how unfair. I would have played flawlessly, if only to put a smile on Eva's cheerless face. I wanted to amaze her with my great talent and make her stop scrubbing what could never be cleaned.

When the music ended, Rona sat quietly, her resentment tamed. She stared down at her hands, lifting each long finger as if, for a moment, appreciating what she could do.

A Singer sewing machine stood by the window. Like the piano, it was ornate, antique, and still in use by both Rona and Eva. I remember the red flowery cotton jersey knit that was about to be cut and become Rona's favorite summer dress. She would wear it so often, the sun and endless washings would fade red into pink.

That dress would feature significantly in ruining my life. I still have it somewhere in the clutter of my garage with old diaries, faded photos and other secrets I can neither face nor throw away.

2

Rona Lubliner wore her first bra at eleven. At the age of twelve she had the curvy figure of a woman and the mind of a natural leader. At thirteen she lost her voice to laryngitis and when it came back, a thin crackle remained, like a violin tune weaved into a piano sonata. Her friends teased her about it mercilessly, called her a frog, then the Rona-voice became something else to envy, another sexy feature on top of all the sex appeal she already had in abundance.

Rona was a trendsetter. She'd help her girlfriends braid their hair or lengthen and curl their eyelashes or use her Singer sewing machine to take in the hem of their skirts. Daniella Levy looked ridiculous in two braids *a la* Rona, when her mousy, stringy hair could only support one. Le'ora's butt was too fleshy for those super short and clingy summer dresses she copied from Rona. And Dorit's eyes resembled twin cockroaches with those unnaturally long and thick eyelashes.

Rona helped her friends do what they wanted, unaware of their adoration, totally oblivious to the envy she inspired.

The boys all had crushes on her. At school, they would climb up on the roof and hang upside down for a glimpse into the girls' lavatories, mostly when Rona was there. Eithan Rosenthal would drag them down one by one and punch some noses.

Eithan was Rona's official boyfriend. He loved her in a mature way, like a real man. But sometimes he'd forget and behave like a normal thirteen-year-old boy. He'd tie her braids together, lick the apple in her lunchbox or chase her around the schoolyard until she was out of breath.

Eithan had a pronounced stutter and serious disciplinary issues. He was a big boy, a head taller than anyone his age, and he moved gracefully on the basketball court. Academically, he was hopeless. Mrs. Schiller didn't miss an opportunity to humiliate him in class. She'd ask him to read out loud, then she'd watch him struggle, stutter, and hesitate, and her skull-like face would contort in a mockery of a smile. Once she demanded that he explain the text after reading it. It was painful to witness his torment. Eithan stared silently at the floor, rivulets of sweat running down both sides of his reddened face. Sweat instead of tears, I thought, because tough boys don't cry.

Teachers and friends assumed he was an idiot and treated him as such.

Eithan's tragedy was being born in the wrong country. Had he lived in the U.S., his passion for basketball would have been respected and cultivated and his stutter wouldn't have mattered. He'd have been wooed by Ivy League universities, maybe even become a star.

Growing up with athletic aspirations in the Israel of the sixties and seventies was a waste, like constantly flushing money down the toilet. Any budding athlete was destined for delinquency and failure. Israel belonged to science geeks. Art and music also counted, but math and physics were essential. And who wouldn't get into occasional trouble if what he or she loved the most was ridiculed by a whole generation of Holocaust-surviving teachers and parents?

His friends constantly made him repeat complex words and asked, "Why do you have to be so stupid?"

Eithan would answer, "I c-c-can't n-not be what I am."

Sometimes they'd ask just to hear that stuttering answer, which, being a good sport all the way, he'd provide willingly. He never complained. He just kept doing what he loved.

"Why do you let them harass you?" I once asked him.

"I give them what they want, Shelli, so they'll expect nothing and let me play ball."

I watched his mouth. "You didn't stutter."

He put a finger to his lips and winked at me, and there was great wisdom in his sparkling eyes. Rona didn't know he could speak normally until much later, but we never had the chance to discuss his pretend affliction because by then she'd stopped talking to me.

As for myself, I was awful in math and physics, but also in sports, which saved me a lot of grief and kept me off the radar. My Israeli-born parents, *sabres*, never had to endure racial discrimination and therefore didn't expect their children to excel in any subject. At least that's how my therapist later explained my mediocrity.

Like Eithan, I'd played my own game. I trained my face in front of the mirror to convey deep concentration. I'd tilt my head left and crinkle my forehead a little. That expression of wonder had been endearing on me as a twelve-year-old. Today I pay for it with vertical lines between my eyebrows, a twinge in my neck and a bad shoulder. Teachers were content with my fake attention and I was left in peace to follow my own interests.

Worlds of fantasy would lure me in, and all included Rona.

I'd easily move from one intricate rescue operation to the next. I'd imagine various ways in which Rona would get hurt, mostly by the massive and virile Eithan. She would come to me for advice, and I would detect a physical trauma—a black eye behind her sunglasses, a long scratch on her white throat concealed by thick make-up. My favorite scenario featured a gunshot wound. I'd sit her down and cleverly pull the truth behind her injury out of her while stopping the bleeding and bandaging her wound.

Then came the concert hall fantasies.

I would become the star, the diva, despite my late start, while Rona Lubliner remained a normal person, another face in my adoring audience. Walking onto the stage to thundering applause, I'd gracefully sit at the gleaming ebony baby grand and make an important face. Since I couldn't imagine my hands actually creating any music, the fantasy would then jump forward to the climax. The last notes of "Appassionata" or "Waldstein" still drifting in the electrified air, I would curtsy elegantly at the standing ovation. As I picked up one of the hundreds of roses thrown at me, smelled it and tossed it into the orchestra, I would glimpse Rona and Eva in the first row—the house seats I'd provided. Eva would be smiling, finally noticing my existence.

It was difficult, forcing my imagination to paint an expression I'd never seen, a smile on Eva's perpetual unhappiness. Rona's smile was easy to imagine. In her case, I had difficulty painting her face with the appropriate magnitude of envy.

I would blow them kisses, and, in my generosity, I'd never mention the cruel lectures Rona had given me about arthritic fingers and how it was too late for me to play the piano.

While my obsession with Rona remained a secret from the world, Eithan's love for her was out in the open and a target for ridicule. The refined Rona excelled in academics and was the complete opposite of the big stuttering boy.

They seemingly had nothing in common, but Rona recognized what I knew and what the rest of them would not see until later: the dignity and the intelligence beyond Eithan's stutter and his hopeless preoccupation with basketball. Rona protected him because Rona saw the promise.

3

On a spring day in the 1970s at eight o'clock in the morning the *z'fira* sounded—an even alarm, unlike the up and down air raid warning signals. In Mrs. Schiller's class, chairs skidded backwards as we all stood up.

I looked out the window onto a street that had become as still as a photograph. Two elderly men at a sidewalk café stopped playing chess, put out their cigarettes and slowly pushed themselves to their feet. Cars stopped on the road and their drivers stepped out to stand unmoving by the open doors. A young woman stopped pushing a stroller, stood still and smiled down at her baby. Other than emergency vehicles and surgeons in the operating room, all activities ceased for one minute.

The z'fira signified the beginning of Yom HaShoah. Holocaust Remembrance Day.

Even the trains stopped in their tracks for one minute on this twenty-seventh day of the Jewish month of Nissan. And no experience was as chilling as being stuck in a packed, stalled train on Holocaust Day.

For one minute we were supposed to devote our thoughts, and the meaning of our existence, to six million of our mothers and fathers, brothers and sisters, who were brutally and systematically murdered by the Nazis in Europe.

When the z'fira sounded, I was transported to a time before my birth, to a place I'd never seen, and into memories that were not my own. I saw myself in the midst of a black and white film, my fate one with old people and children in dark coats on their way to the camps. In my head, and for that one minute, their faces became those of my friends and family.

The emotional minute triggered my fantasies.

In the spirit of the day, I pictured myself hiding Rona, my beloved, under my bed, protecting her with my body from the Nazi soldiers and their bayonets. Yet I immediately abandoned that story line. It was ludicrous, since they'd also be after me. I switched the villain to a raging, crazy Eva, a mop in her hands, shouting, "*Molto vibrato!*"

When I looked around at my classmates, I noticed that some of them were giggling, possibly thinking of their breakfast, football or a new pair of blue jeans. Little Daniella Levy was crying, taken by the moment or by something unrelated but equally moving.

Rona was examining her hands, each finger separately, as she did after performing a piano piece. She seemed so tense, I expected her to bolt and run out of class before the minute was over. She hated the drama about horrors that happened so long ago. When you're twelve, thirty years seem like three hundred. She loathed the depressing cello music on the radio, the fact that you had to drop everything and stand still.

"Why can't we be a normal country," she'd say, "have big staircases in our houses, like the Brady Bunch, and live football and cheerleaders?"

I'd heard stories of the Holocaust from early childhood; I ate those stories with a spoon. Rona was force fed with a shovel.

"My mother's milk was laced with the poison of shoah," she'd say.

Where was Eithan that day?

He usually had such presence in class, his size alone made him noticeable. That day he didn't show up.

A Small Country about to Vanish

When the minute of silence was over, we all sat down, still solemn. Mrs. Schiller, thin and as upright as a broomstick—and damaged from the shoah, like many of her contemporaries—pointed with a long, crooked finger at Gidi Ishbitzky and demanded, "Talk to me about Eithan."

Gidi swallowed hard. "About the Holocaust?"

"About Eithan," Schiller said, "Didn't he give you a bloody nose?"

On the previous day, a fight had broken out on the basketball court. Eithan Rosenthal argued a point with Asher Schwartz and Gidi Ishbitzky. They exchanged blows, and Gidi was taken to the school nurse with a messy nosebleed. Others were involved, but Eithan's blow was the most effective.

"Well, he punched me," Gidi said, "but we made up. Why?"

"His *schticks* have to stop," she said.

I noticed the piece of paper in her hand, which she folded and unfolded, as if unable to make up her mind whether or not to share it with us. I recognized the ruled page that had been torn out of Daniella's notebook. I knew what it was. We all knew. The classroom filled with gasps of horror. How did she get hold of it?

The paper crackled in her hands as she elaborated on what we already knew, about Eithan's mother, an immigrant widow from Romania who was raising three boys on her own.

"Even she has given up on trying to control him. He'll have to go to a special school."

Schiller turned the paper around. It was a nude caricature —very well drawn—with huge breasts, legs far apart and a skull-like face that could only be Schiller's own.

"I found this in Eithan's backpack," she said. "He claimed it wasn't his work. Which one of you has drawn this masterpiece? Asher Schwartz?"

Asher shook his head no.

"And didn't Eithan hit you too?"

Asher willingly told of a fight he'd lost to Eithan. He was happy to get off the subject of the drawing because his girlfriend was the artist.

"Daniella Levy," Schiller said.

Daniella shivered in response. I thought she'd own up, but instead she told Schiller how Eithan once tied her braids together around a pole.

Daniella, who would constantly doodle during lectures, had ripped the page out of her spiral notebook and passed it around for all of us to enjoy. Then the bell had announced the end of the school day. Eithan, being the last holding the drawing, shoved it into his backpack, only to be stopped by Schiller on the way out. I guessed she confiscated it then.

"For the last time, whose work is it?" she insisted. "The artist will confess, or Eithan takes the blame. I've been looking for an excuse to kick him out of school."

We sneaked peeks at Daniella, who said nothing.

Schiller continued her interrogation. She didn't give up and eventually everyone said something. Not about the drawing, but rather about Eithan, who wasn't there to speak for himself. Boys and girls, supposedly his friends, told stories such as "Yesterday at the drinking fountain, Eithan pushed my face into the water" and "He kicked my butt three weeks ago in gym class."

Some tales were so complicated, they put my own fantasies to shame.

Mrs. Schiller used to tell us horror stories about her life in Nazi Germany, of how she had to hide, silent and in a standing position, behind a double wall for almost a year. We decided that was the reason she walked erect and rigid, her feet in the ten-to-two position, as if never having left the inside of that double wall. She'd made up for her year of silence by

A Small Country about to Vanish

frequently lecturing her students about how lucky and spoiled they were.

Whenever Schiller reminisced about her past, Rona would excuse herself and take a long bathroom break. She told me that having to listen to her mother's Hungarian rhapsodies had drained her of sympathy.

"Shelli Kahana, what do you have to say about Eithan?"

It was my turn. I had my own problems with this hateful woman. My failing grades proved that my head was mostly in the clouds. I was hoping to please her with a good enough story about Eithan that she'd let me return to my fantasies of musical glory and rescue operations.

My only grievances were that Eithan Rosenthal ignored me because he loved Rona and that she preferred him over me because he was a boy. I wanted his banishment, so I brought up an old incident—Eithan's bike colliding with mine—which had actually been my fault.

As I spoke, waves of disapproval steamed off Rona.

When I was done, I expected Rona to take the stage. Her confession was going to nail him good, because we all knew how she did all his homework and still, he made her life a misery. He'd chase her around the schoolyard until she cried, pull on her braids and, despite her resistance, kiss her on the mouth.

Rona remained silent. Her long and thick black braids rested on her chest, and in my eyes she was the beautiful Indian princess, Tiger Lily, waiting proudly for her execution by Captain Hook.

I nudged her. Our classmates, thirsty for blood now they'd tasted it, joined me in urging Rona. Her round freckled face turned bright red, but her lips remained white horizontal lines. She refused the spotlight.

"Come on." I made such a fuss, Schiller's eyes narrowed on Rona.

She waddled toward us, the aura of a double wall moving her from side to side all the way to our desk. She shoved the drawing in Rona's face.

"Do you know who did this?"

"What's the big deal?" Rona blurted out. "Lots of artists draw naked people."

Schiller glared at Rona through thick glasses.

"Was it Eithan?"

Rona stared down at her long magical fingers. Her voice was cracklier than usual when she said, "I don't like your witch hunt, and I'm not going to add twigs to your fire today of all days."

A Small Country about to Vanish

4

I expected Schiller to explode in anger and demand that Rona leave the room, but Rona, a straight-A student, was untouchable. Schiller briefly narrowed her eyes, as if battling a memory. Then she ripped up the drawing and threw the tiny pieces into the wastepaper basket.

Daniella Levy winced at the sight of her destroyed masterpiece, a reaction that should have given her away. Schiller missed it.

Schiller waddled back to the world map on the wall. She pointed at the Sahara region and started teaching a normal geography lesson, as if nothing significant had just occurred. At that she was excellent, teaching us facts we had to memorize and rules we had to stick by. Facts and rules and nothing about decency.

I don't like your witch hunt, and I'm not going to add twigs to your fire today of all days.

Rona's words sounded so noble, so enlightened, I had another reason to love and envy her. She didn't yet have the maturity to speak of injustice, but she knew enough not to contribute to it. She'd had the courage to stand up to her teacher and above the fickle mob.

On Holocaust Remembrance Day the year I turned thirteen, Rona was my real teacher. She could handle people like Schiller. Both authority figures in her life—her teacher and her mother—had been hardened by the same events.

Did Schiller learn anything? Probably not. Learning from one's student required a humility she didn't know existed.

Humiliation, yes. That she had experienced and that she could inflict in abundance. Schiller, tormented in and by her past, should have avoided persecuting others. She would have accomplished so much more had she commented on the quality of that caricature, praised the artist, suggested changes, then admitted that her feelings were hurt. Daniella would have learned to own up to her work.

The subject of sending Eithan to a special school never came up again. He remained with the class, always next to Rona and competing with me for her attention. He graduated with the rest of us. I give him a lot of credit for sticking with so-called friends who had betrayed him.

The moral of that story?

Eva Lubliner may have embarrassed Rona with her hollering but somehow in that angry language, she taught her daughter more than the discipline of hitting a set of keys every afternoon from four to six.

Eva didn't embrace all music. In her blind hatred for all things German post-nineteenth century, she'd forbidden Richard Wagner in her home.

Naturally—for what's a teenager without rebellion?—Rona developed an obsession for the controversial, anti-Semitic composer. She wanted to own a Wagner, any Wagner. We went shopping for music.

Finding recordings of Wagner's operas turned out to be quite an ordeal in the Israel of the 1970s. One store owner behaved like we were asking for a copy of *Mein Kampf*.

"We don't sell Nazi filth here," he said. "But the *mamzer* by the butcher's shop does."

The mamzer—son of a bitch—owned the large record store on Dizengoff Street that sold Rona her first copy of *Tristan ünd Isolde*.

Rona didn't particularly like the harsh music at first, but she learned it by heart and eventually it grew on her. She would sing it out loud, exaggerating the crackle in her voice, making both me and Eithan laugh by twisting her freckled face and crossing her violet eyes. She could follow all the convoluted motives of the opera: ecstasy, love-glance, love-death and transfiguration.

She once explained the third act to Eithan and me.

"Isolde's swan song is called the 'Liebestod.' She kneels by the fallen body of Tristan, and, in her ecstasy, she sees him rising alive before her. She sinks, apparently lifeless, onto Tristan's corpse. It seems like double suicide, but if you listen to the score, she actually goes through *Verklärung*, transfiguration. You see? Isolde doesn't really die, although it appears that way."

"G-good. I w-was wo-worried," Eithan said. "Let's call our first b-born Isolde."

Rona had taught herself the German language, also to spite Eva.

"Ima would kill me if she knew," she said, a lavender glint of mischief in her eyes.

She could read the German fashion magazines and would dress all of us. We bought the material and she'd make our clothes on her old Singer.

Around the same time, Rona bought three identical pewter rings in a jewelry store and called them *Der Nibelüngen*. Eithan and I each got one. I loved my hideous ring. It featured a warrior maiden, the Valkyrie. Eithan wore his on his pinky finger for a whole year, then lost it in a camping trip near Masada, maybe on purpose. Rona and I wore those rings for a long time. I still wear mine.

Eithan Rosenthal didn't care one way or another about opera, but he would take a break from basketball practice and indulge Rona, sharing that guilty pleasure with her when her parents weren't home. I say her parents, when really only Eva counted. Rona had a father, I'm sure. A pair of huge slippers in the corner suggested his existence, slippers that could not have belonged to Eva, Rona or her little brother, Uri. Mr. Lubliner existed, but I don't remember him. His wife's overwhelming presence had reduced him to a pair of empty house shoes.

When we studied theories in astrophysics, Rona grasped something essential about her mother.

"Ima's intense gravitational force sucks in everything within her reach. Her soul is a black hole made of the broken pieces of her murdered loved ones. Their lights are her darkness."

Eva Lubliner was a mystery to me. I would've made a better student than Rona, piano and otherwise. I would have absorbed her stories like the sponges she used for the floor. I had so many questions for her.

My mother was of Eva's generation but her complete opposite. As a typical sabre, Mom had never experienced persecution. I guessed that was the reason she'd kept her youthful voice and appearance and her easy-going attitude.

"What could the Jews have done to save themselves, Ima?" I asked, my eyes bleary from a night of non-stop reading. "Why didn't they pack their bags and cross the border to Switzerland at the first sight of those *Juden Verboten* signs on restaurants? The swastikas on shop windows, weren't those good enough alarm clocks? The transfer into ghettos?"

My mother sucked on her first cigarette of the morning and sipped her Turkish coffee.

"No one believed that the country of Beethoven, so civilized and cultured, would allow genocide," she said.

A Small Country about to Vanish

"What about the German locals?" I was close to tears. "Why didn't they stop the rounding-up of their Jewish neighbors?"

"Some helped," Mom said, "like the family who gave your Mrs. Schiller a place to hide. People could smell the smoke billowing from the crematoria and see the ashes in the air and on the ground." Ashes from her cigarette fell to the table as if to stress her point. "Still no one knew exactly what was happening. Or they knew and were simply following orders, afraid to speak up. Don't worry, Shelli," she added. "Now we have a homeland, such atrocities will never happen again."

"Would you have known the signs of danger?" I picked at what had kept me up at night.

"I may have known," she said. "I know the danger of this thing." She raised the cigarette. "I cough every morning, but do I stop?"

"That's not the same, because you choose to smoke," I argued. "If we're so smart, why are we so stupid about the hints?"

My father overheard us.

"Don't blame the victims, Shelli," he said.

This was hopeless. My parents weren't authorities on the subject, and I needed answers.

Mrs. Schiller would have known. Hadn't she spent a whole year inside that double wall with nothing to do but think? Yet asking Schiller was out of the question. She scared me.

Eva Lubliner had been wise enough to pack herself up and leave before it all happened. Before the killings. Before the exterminations. She'd read the signs *and* she'd acted on them. She would've been able to teach me how to save myself if the shoah were to happen again. I so wanted to ask her, but I was afraid she'd totally miss the point because of her poor Hebrew. I could imagine her yelling, "*Staccato, staccatissimo,*" or worse, throwing a sponge at me and expecting me to get down on my knees and mop along with her while Rona played sonatas.

That puzzle constantly gnawed at me. Having no one to ask —those who knew were too crazy—I kept checking books out of the library, then I'd stay up and read all night. I wanted to pinpoint the exact moment in history, in that heating of the political atmosphere, at which those victims could have saved themselves and their loved ones.

What force had kept the Jewish people in their expensive Berlin and Leipzig homes, playing their pianos and violins, until it was too late to get out? A Jewish doctor suddenly barred from practicing—what had kept him there?

Don't blame the victims.

As I read, both fiction and non-fiction, the trend of history had revealed itself to me. It was so obvious. The nomadic Jews would be welcomed into a starving country—Poland, Germany or Hungary—encouraged to immigrate in order to improve the host's economy. In time they would thrive and with them, the rest of the population.

History constantly repeated itself. Its big grinding wheel might slow down or speed up, but there was always a click of warning at similar points at the turning of the wheel. The Jews were deaf to that click. Sometimes their proverbial finger would get caught in the wheel's spokes. They'd simply put a Band-Aid on it and ignore the next click.

When starving people lost their hunger, their eyes opened and they saw a tribe of aliens who posed as humans—loud, self-assured and a few steps ahead of them. The Jews would start getting on their nerves with their intellectual behavior, with their maddening habit of being successful in business. Anti-Semitism would begin to flourish, first beneath the surface, nothing obvious. But instead of packing the

A Small Country about to Vanish

Stradivarius, the Erard and their Picassos at the first painted swastika, or even leaving it all behind and saving only their families, the Jews would participate in political activism, the shrill kind that irritated the fascists or the communists. They'd get arrested. The hate would flow. Concentration camps would follow.

We were so book clever, I thought, but so extremely stupid when it came to learning from our own history.

I got more from reading all night than during the day in school.

Mrs. Schiller had completely missed the meaning of being a teacher. Instead of describing in detail the humiliating year she had spent inside the double wall—eating, sleeping and crapping where she stood—she should have been teaching us how to avoid having to hide in the first place.

Instead of telling us of the past, she should have been teaching us for the future.

Instead of useless facts about the natural resources of the Sahara—and other places we couldn't visit for diplomatic reasons—she should have taught us about the political history she had experienced firsthand. About how to recognize the signs and run before the exits were barred.

I was most affected by one novelist, Yehiel Dinur, whose entire family was murdered in Auschwitz. The pen name he had chosen for himself, Ka-Tsetnik 135633, meant Concentration Camper in Yiddish. I'd read all his novels in a row, like a chain-smoker of books. Now, years later, I remember only snippets from each and they all run together.

He'd arrived in Israel before it was officially Israel, alone and guilt-ridden for outliving his loved ones but with a sense of a mission. There he decided that he'd survived in order to write the truth as an eyewitness and to bring his family back to life in books. Ka-Tsetnik believed that among his kind, he would

35

meet sympathy and understanding. He was in for another horror he hadn't expected.

As he rode a crowded bus in Tel Aviv, carrying his finished manuscript, he thought of a wholly different ride, a train to Auschwitz. In his loneliness, he craved contact with his fellow human beings. Their occasional touch reminded him that he still lived. But people on the packed Israeli bus did their best to avoid his incidental closeness, even resenting him for invading their physical space.

When he tried to publish his first novel, one publisher claimed, "We already have enough books about those stories." The publisher didn't even refer to it as the Holocaust. The hard-to-believe tales were just starting to trickle into the country with the survivors. The magnitude of the calamity hadn't yet become common knowledge.

I was taken with Ka-Tsetnik's observations, with his lurid novel-memoirs some dismissed as Holocaust pulp fiction. The worst of his personal horrors wasn't necessarily what he had lost, but the indifference of those he'd expected to embrace him.

For a while I lived and breathed Ka-Tsetnik 135633. I knew his characters, as he had indeed brought them to life with details stark and shocking. In *House of Dolls* he told about his little sister. A Nazi officer used her as a field whore—*feld-hure* was inscribed in a tattoo on her chest. That same officer had a daughter her age and he was the most caring, loving father. After work he tended his beautiful garden and thought nothing of the day's atrocities.

I read voraciously all night and fell asleep in school between my usual episodes of daydreaming.

An Auschwitz survivor tells his loving Israeli-born wife about his life in the death camp. The wife, touched by his stories of starvation, develops a bottomless hunger and starts eating uncontrollably. As an obese woman, her life becomes a roller coaster of overeating and guilt. A man insults her in the street. *Sherman tank*, he calls her when she blocks his path. Realizing that the only way to break the unrelenting cycle is escape, she leaves Israel for the United States. A year later she returns to her country and her husband, slim and beautiful again.

I convinced Rona to read this book, and it was the only one on the subject of the Holocaust she ever finished.

My mother heard me crying one night. She barged into my room without knocking, plucked the book I was reading—*Salamandra*—from my hands, and said, "That's it, Shelli."

She picked up book after book off the mountain on the floor and read their titles. "Enough Ka-Tsetnik."

"I'm just trying to understand," I argued.

"No, you're trying to *live* it," she said.

The next morning she returned all the books to the library and left the librarian with instructions about what I could and couldn't read.

Still, with Rona's help, I kept reading my favorite author. I'd send her to the library to check the books out and she'd keep them for me in her room next to her Wagner. Ka-Tsetnik became my banned author, my rebellion.

The wheels of time turned.

We were fifteen. Eithan, Rona and I would sit on her narrow bed. I would read by the light of the lamp—a huge, green glass bottle covered by a macramé shade Rona had knotted as a personal tribute to the seventies. Next to me, Rona and Eithan would cuddle and kiss to the sounds of the high-strung German opera.

Rona would sing Isolde's words in her crackly voice. "*Seht ihr's, Freunde? Seht ihr's nicht?*" Can't you see, my friends? Do you not see (how wonderful he is)?

Rona didn't seem to mind my presence.

And Eithan? I don't know what he thought of me being with them as he romanced Rona, but I have a flicker of a memory.

Isolde was screeching her love-death song. Eithan's hand slipped through Rona's dress and, for a split second, our fingertips touched at the clasp of her bra. Then the clasp opened, his eyes met mine in the dim light thrown by the macramé shade, and I knew that he knew he was sharing Rona with me.

A Small Country about to Vanish

5.

Thirty-five years later, that fifteen-year-old girl obsessed with the shoah is no more. I can't bring myself to read any of those books. To dwell on what had consumed me as a child.

My home is in Los Angeles. I'm amicably divorced with two grown children. My son is studying to be a lawyer at UCLA. My daughter, Thalma, lives with me. She's an out-of-work actress who waits tables at a local bar with the hope of being discovered. In her free time she wears a pink motorcycle helmet and races up and down the Malibu canyons with her biking buddies. In my case, both apples fell far from the tree.

I'd bought a beach-front house because I'd always wanted to take a steaming-hot cup of coffee from my own kitchen, walk barefoot to the sand, and find that the coffee was still steaming hot by the time I got to the ocean. Drinking hot coffee on the sand was an expensive luxury.

Against my living room wall stands an antique upright piano. Just like Rona's piano, it is ebony with burgundy accents, holds silver candlesticks, and has an ivory keyboard and an ornamented gold engraving that says, *Erard, Paris*. It needs tuning, at least I think it does. How would I know, and why should I care, as neither I nor my kids can play it? I'd bought it online for three thousand dollars, plus one thousand shipping and handling, although it wasn't handled very well. One of the silver candlesticks fell off in transit and I had to Super-Glue it back on.

The piano, like my beach house, is an extravagance I can't really afford. According to the seller, who had shipped it to me straight from Israel, the piano's former owners were deceased. I couldn't bring myself to ask who the former owners were.

I draw the curtains every afternoon to protect my Erard from sunlight, then I polish it until it squeaks, the way my daughter and her Hells Angels buddies polish their Harleys. This is as close as I can get to that relentless childhood longing of being a famous concert pianist with lovers all over the world, roses in every hotel room, applause in concert halls, and rave reviews for my masterful interpretation of Rachmaninoff.

I still can't make music, and the keyboard I use, my writing keyboard, is more forgiving. It allows errors and doesn't mind the stiffness of older fingers.

When I moved away from Israel, I took my fantasyland with me. I still live in it, but now my intricate stories pay the bills.

Some days I'm a Rona dreamer again. Those stories don't fill my wallet, but they satisfy in other ways.

And I wonder where she is today.

I never saw her name anywhere in the music world, and I searched well—under Lubliner, in case she still used her maiden name, and under Rosenthal, in case she'd married Eithan. I can still imagine her, still tell myself stories. Still picture her as she was, a child becoming a woman.

Israel is always in the news. Suicide bombs rock this restaurant or that in Haifa, Tel Aviv or Jerusalem. I travel often to Tel Aviv. On one of my visits to see my aging parents, I was reading *Ha'aretz* and a small ad caught my eye. *Piano lessons, all ages, all levels. Call Rona.*

That stung. What happened to the rule about being too old after three? What about the supple fingers and the clean-slate brain?

I dialed the number. A smoke-saturated, tired voice on the answering machine instructed me to leave a message. The voice had a familiar crackle in it. It could have been anyone with that crackly voice and that common name, Rona. My heart racing, I quickly hung up. I immediately called again just to give the voice a face. I tore off the ad and shoved it into my purse between two photos of my children.

Since that day, I thought of Rona often.

I'd seen her, imagined a glimpse here and there in gestures and sounds made by others. I'd seen her in Tel Aviv, New York and Los Angeles, in airports, in bookstores, in coffee shops. Since I don't know what she looks like today, she'd take different forms in my imaginings.

I recently had dinner with Thalma in a restaurant on Santa Monica Boulevard. A rowdy group celebrated in the back of the room. The day was June 17, Rona Lubliner's birthday. I zoomed in on a slim, fashionable woman about my age who stood up to make a speech. Her short skirt showed off beautiful legs. Pushing fifty in a skinny mini, I thought. I held my breath. A face, a figure, even a mind can change, but not the legs. That maybe-Rona was laughing out loud in a smoke-saturated voice, obviously the life of that little party.

I'd seen her countless times at sidewalk cafés on the trendy Dizengoff Street in Tel Aviv, sipping cappuccino with a group of adoring friends. Sometimes she'd resemble the girl she used to be—long black braids, a tight, pinkish-red, flowery sundress, a backpack, flat sandals with thin straps.

I knew that was silly, expecting a woman in her late forties to wear the same braids she'd worn as a teen. Besides, that faded sundress had ended up in my garage.

Rona is different each time I spot her, and she never sees me. Her states of happiness and social status vary, but what captures my attention is that touch of sadness, that pride in the way she carries herself, that defiant flinging of what used to be a braid, and now is only air, over her shoulder.

When I'm alone at home and in that rare state of writing with complete abandon, I often hear the ghost of a sonata played on my piano. I pretend that Rona is upstairs in my sunny living room, playing for old times' sake. I sometimes sneak upstairs, just to make sure I'm truly alone, but then the magic breaks, the music stops and all I can hear is the very real street below—drunks leaving the bars at the end of the alley with songs on their lips, or kids squealing while rollerblading down the steep slope of the street toward the Pacific Ocean.

Once I tiptoed upstairs and saw her sitting at my piano wearing a pink dress and Tiger Lily braids. When I blinked, she was gone.

Shaken, I took out the yellowing ad and dialed the number.

"Shalom," said a crackly, very familiar voice.

I couldn't speak. I was out of breath. I ran a caressing hand across the worn-out wooden surface of my Erard and hung up. She probably would've done it first had she known it was me.

Despite my habit of making up stories and changing real events by imagining them differently, I can do nothing about the memory of an incident that nearly cost me my life but was no more than a blip on the radar of Rona's busy social life.

I never think of the day Rona stopped talking to me altogether. If a thought surfaces, I quickly push it away, lest it bring back the darkness, the smell of disinfectants, the heaving stomach, the nightmares of a gas chamber filled with Zyclon B.

6

One afternoon Rona played a Wagner polka because Eva wasn't home. Fighter jets continuously zoomed over our heads as this was 1973 and a bitter war raged at the borders. Those jets didn't bother Rona. She kept playing, and I kept listening through a series of supersonic booms. Then the booms were over and she stopped midnote, something she'd never done before. She claimed that interrupting a piece of music was like killing the dead composer all over again.

But that day she'd stopped. "His dance music is like a death march," she said in a low tone. She swiveled around on her black stool to face me, shocking me again by saying, "I'm floating in emptiness and great loneliness. My holidays are sad, my family is small—only the four of us. I have no *dod* or *dodda*, no *saba* or *savta*. I don't even know where they're buried in Europe. When I grow up I'll have a large family like yours and huge Pessah dinners."

"My family is yours," I said, touched.

"But I'm not theirs," she said.

Our friendship died when we were sixteen. Viciously murdered, more like, and left to shrivel up and dry in the unforgiving Israeli sun. No *Kaddish* was said, no proper burial, no headstone was given me on which to place wild flowers and light a *yahrzeit* candle.

Sometimes at sunset I pour myself a glass of Yarden Cabernet on my balcony, look out to the Pacific Ocean and toast my friendship with Rona Lubliner, long dead but still the most intimate I'd ever had.

Two things changed for me when our friendship died.

The first, I stopped reading about the Holocaust. I completely divorced myself from that subject and couldn't even talk about it.

The second, the claustrophobic nightmares began. I'd be trapped in a small space, unable to see. I'd paw my way in the dark. I'd touch a craggy wall and start banging on it, trying to break my way through. I'd scratch it with my fingernails. I could hear others next to me, doing the same thing. The place smelled of a harsh disinfectant. I'd feel the burn in my lungs and wake up struggling for breath, covered in sweat.

The family doctor started treating me for asthma. Since then I always keep an inhaler with me. The nightmares, while less frequent, come in clusters nowadays and are only related to memories of Rona.

My parents never found out the reason why Rona and I parted ways. As far as they knew, I made new friends whose interests were closer to mine.

We *could* have drifted apart naturally. By the time we were sixteen, Rona had a new set of friends—*hev're*—the daredevils, the active, outdoorsy, camping type who slept in the desert among snakes and scorpions, rappelled down cliffs in the Golan Heights, rafted down angry rivers and jumped out of airplanes without opening their parachutes till the last minute. I preferred the company of those who lived dangerously only in their heads—the writers and the artists.

As it happened, there was no gradual drifting apart. Our breakup was rude and abrupt and ruinous.

After that, in the course of the last two and a half years of high school, Rona and I exchanged exactly three words. Actually only two, considering we spoke Hebrew.

Those exact words were *Excuse me* and *sorry*.

I'd been engrossed in conversation in the crowded school hallway and didn't see Rona approaching. Her curt, crackly voice was a sudden presence in my ear.

"*Sliha.*"

Since Hebrew doesn't differentiate *forgive* from *excuse*, I mistook her word for an apology while she was only asking me to get out of her way. She said "*sliha*" in the same irritated voice she would use when grumbling at her mother.

I wanted to ask, *Does Eva still annoy you, and which of your new friends has to hear about it, rappelling Dorit or skydiving Nathaniel?*

Instead, I replied, "*Sliha,*" meaning *forgive me*.

I'd flattened myself against the wall to let Rona by. As she passed, her elbow accidentally brushed against my side. It was a hot, dry day, and a spark of electricity sizzled between us. I kept touching that tingling spot so often that day, a friend asked if I had a belly ache.

Rona and Eithan remained inseparable during high school. On chance meetings with me, he'd greet me cordially, a little glint in his eyes that said, *I won the prize*. Rona couldn't even look at me.

At eighteen we all joined the IDF, *Tzahal*, in various duties and capacities, forcing me—allowing me?—to completely lose touch with my former classmates. The last I'd heard, both Rona and Eithan served in dangerous military posts.

Had Eithan eventually left his ungrateful homeland for a place in which his talent was respected? Is Rona playing for pennies in a nightclub or teaching piano, the writer of that yellowing ad I keep in my purse?

Since the Hebrews are nomads by nature, Rona may have gone back to Hungary, to where her mother's family lived and died en masse, to prove that Jews still played the piano, like in the Hasidic song "Am Israel Hai." The people of Israel live.

She may be living alone in a rented room in Budapest, subjected daily to the language that had haunted her childhood, trying to reconcile with it. She could be teaching piano lessons to Hungarian children who are entranced by her because she's the only Jew they know.

Since the Hungarians, the Poles, or the Germans for that matter, don't know their own history—who would want to know such history?—the young generation has become fascinated with the Jewish people who look and sound exotic and interesting. The young generation don't know any because their grandparents, who mass-murdered them, also erased the memory of their existence.

Rona may have been given a scholarship to study music in Berlin. It had been the seventies, and Germany, in the name of its former Nazis, had been making amends with the European Jews by paying damages, at least for stolen property. It was impossible to compensate for six million lost lives, but Rona may have won that scholarship for her talents and because of her mother's losses. She would have been excited at the opportunity to study music in Wagner's country of origin, only to have Eva say in Hungarian, "You have no business going back to that Jewish mass grave called Europe."

Maybe the scholarship had fallen through because Eithan Rosenthal insisted on getting married and having babies right away and Rona caved because he was the love of her life.

So many maybes concerning Rona and Eithan. All I have is maybes.

For all I know, either one of them, or both, lost their lives during their military service or years later in a *pigua* while simply shopping for groceries.

Pigua.

The Hebrew word for a suicide bombing is short, soft sounding, non-specific. In the Alcalay dictionary, *pigua* only means *an obstacle*. The dictionary was written long before Palestinian martyrs had started blowing themselves up in ice cream parlors, and a new word hasn't been invented yet.

Is Rona Lubliner the deceased former owner of my old Erard?

Despite our disastrous parting, I'd rather imagine her alive, happy or not, and hope that she sometimes thinks of me.

7

Rona Lubliner-Rosenthal often regrets having given up that music scholarship. She and Eithan had no choice but to marry very young since she was pregnant with Tally, now twenty-eight and with a rapidly growing family of her own.

The Rosenthals live in plenty, good health and apparent happiness in the affluent Savyon—the Beverly Hills of Tel Aviv. The modest Rona feels somewhat shy about her pretentious address and when strangers ask where she lives, she says, "near Yahud."

Eithan feels entitled and proud of his achievements. He gave up his basketball dreams, his stutter and his volatile temper long ago, surprising everyone who knew him by making it big in the computer business. Israel became the Silicon Valley of the Middle East, and Eithan made millions in a few years.

The Rosenthal's house is an old renovated Tuscan-style villa with a rose garden in the front and seventeen ancient olive trees in the back. Those generous trees bear fruit every other year. Rona learned from her housekeeper, Jihan—a warm and dignified Arab woman who has seven children—how to press the olives for extra virgin oil and how to preserve the olives in jars. Her friends and family consider those pickled olives a delicacy. Rona keeps the recipe a secret; it is her only claim to fame. A turquoise ceramic hand—a *hamsa*—hangs on the wall by the entrance, a gift from Jihan meant to protect Rona's home and family from the evil eye. The hand isn't exactly

A Small Country about to Vanish

Rona's style, but she keeps it there so as not to hurt Jihan's feelings.

Rona's beautiful living room has her dream staircase, like in the house of the Brady Bunch, her favorite childhood show. The room is filled with thousands of books Rona has read and Eithan hasn't, and big art. Enormous, monochromatic abstract canvases featuring ample use of crushed quartz, parts of weaved ropes, broken chains and, for contrast, white feathers.

All the art pieces were created—some recently, some years ago—by up-and-coming and fashionable Daniella Schwartz, who happens to be Daniella Levy from their school days, an artist who nowadays makes sure she signs and owns up to all her artwork.

Daniella is married to her childhood sweetheart, Dr. Asher Schwartz, also an old friend of the Rosenthals.

Eva Lubliner's ancient piano adorns the corner by the kitchen, along with her old Singer sewing machine, both at rest and serving as quaint decoration. Rona and her children prefer playing the Steinway, an acoustic, contemporary ebony baby grand.

There's no replacement for the Singer sewing machine, on which Rona and her mother used to make and mend the family's clothes. The Rosenthals don't bother with mending anything, and they buy only designer fashions.

It's late Friday night and, like other Israeli homes, Rona and Eithan's place becomes a mini political headquarters. Good friends from early childhood get together for dinner, drinks and soccer on TV. This Friday is sandwiched between two significant Tuesdays. The previous Tuesday was Yom HaShoah, Holocaust Remembrance Day. The following Tuesday will be Yom HaZikaron, Memorial Day for the fallen soldiers.

Solemnity aside, tonight they're gathered in front of the huge TV. They cheer while the Israeli soccer team beats the Russians four to one. They know their team will never get near the World Cup, so this small triumph over the Russians serves more as reassurance of their nation's value among other nations. The street outside is alive with celebration. People are laughing and dancing, waving blue and white flags, popping champagne corks and sounding their car horns.

This politically isolated country craves being part of the world, craves being more than a military target for its immediate neighbors or a constant target for European condemnation. This country is fed up with its excellence being limited to military operations and, well, its abundance of piano and violin virtuosos.

In the Rosenthals' living room, the excitement dies fairly quickly. No one but Eithan is a true soccer fan. They start discussing contemporary events and arguing, even when they agree with each other, because conflicts and self-doubts are the essence of life.

Eithan towers over his friends, fifty next year, and still graceful and muscular, with a head full of gorgeous white hair and loud, healthy laughter. Rona is thirty kilos overweight, ten for each pregnancy. She is dressed in all-black Donna Karan.

Rona tries not to get involved in the political arguments but as she picks at the food in the kitchen—not really eating, just making sure it's hot enough or cold enough before serving it—she hears snippets of heated conversation. The three in the living room are yelling at each other like barbarians, yelling and not listening.

"Keep the Golan Heights, the West Bank and East Jerusalem," Asher Schwartz says. "Keep the West Bank settlements, all of it."

A Small Country about to Vanish

Eithan's voice booms. "This government needs someone with balls, like Golda."

Daniella Schwartz tries to cool down the discussion. "Did you guys hear the latest about Gidi and Le'ora Ishbitzky?" she asks. "They just opened a second shopping center in Warsaw."

They chat about others who are becoming rich and successful in Eastern Europe. Rappelling Dorit plays the violin in the Berlin Philharmonic. She obviously has a thing for taut ropes and strings. Another acquaintance will sing Verdi this spring in the Vienna opera house.

The new Israelis are excited by this opportunity to revisit Eastern Europe. Trips to the death camps are now open to all, and even so, their children are quickly forgetting the Holocaust. Some haven't even heard of Anne Frank.

When Rona was growing up, the shoah was still raw and recent, still in the air, inhaled with every breath. She and her friends learned about it from the freshly wounded—teachers, parents, authors of books. Today the youngest survivors are in their midseventies, the most systematic genocide has been written into textbooks and, as ancient history, its horrors are diluted and less horrifying. Rona's own children have learned the fate of their distant relatives with certain indifference, as they had the fate of the Jews under the Roman rule.

What does it have to do with us? they ask. Although they aren't strangers to physical danger—war and suicide bombings—they know nothing about the humiliation and persecution of being a loathed minority.

And Rona believes they shouldn't know.

She stands in her huge, sparkling clean kitchen, gleaming pots and pans dangling over her head, and recalls an old friend whom she had tried to block from her memory, but never could. Shelli's nose was always in books about the Jews and their history, and she would surface when Rona heard those arguments in her own living room.

Shelli would develop theories about why the Jewish people, collectively, are both smart and stupid.

One of those complex theories didn't make sense to Rona when she was younger, but it did now. It had something to do with a wheel and its clicking notches. About history repeating itself. And, yes, how there was always a click of warning at similar points in the wheel's turning, but the loud Jews were too inundated with background noise to hear that certain click. They were always playing their pianos and violins, or arguing politics, and their own racket prevented them from hearing other necessary sounds.

Shelli would have made a big deal about Gidi and Le'ora Ishbitzky and their business endeavors in the new Poland. This is the twenty-first century, Shelli would have said, and the creaky wheel of history has just about clicked into the notch of welcoming the Jews into Eastern Europe. We all know what will come next.

Ah, the cake.

Rona opens the refrigerator—Sub-Zero with extra compartments and a special section for drinks—takes out the cake and uncovers it. The chocolate glazing looks utterly delicious. The slim Daniella won't touch it, but the others will. The kids and their friends would devour it in no time.

What else did Shelli use to say?

She'd been different and a little out there and ahead of her time. She would have pointed out, would have lectured all of them in the living room, about how the smart-stupid Hebrew nomads are now at the chapter of enjoying the glamor and ignoring the first signs of hate. Current events declare that the Europeans love you now because you help their economy, but soon they'll get tired of you and your prosperity and start *kristallnachting* shop windows.

Here, watch the first swastikas. The first blown-up synagogue.

Rona imagines that someone could argue that this time it's different because the Christians don't hate them anymore. It is the Muslims who are taking over Europe and the world.

As if it matters who does the hating, and so openly.

When Rona carries the chocolate cake into the living room, the air is thick with cigarette smoke. In spite of the popularity of cigarettes, lung malignancies are rare in Israel by default.

"Statistically speaking, we have a greater chance of dying of *butterfly*," Asher says, puffing smoke rings toward Eithan and Rona's soaring white ceiling.

Asher knows his statistics. In the Tel-Hashomer medical center, Asher Schwartz is a famous pulmonologist, specializing in blast lung injuries, typical in high-explosive detonations, in which a characteristic butterfly pattern reveals itself on the chest X-ray.

Asher starts talking again about the settlements in the West Bank.

Rona pours Asher's coffee, choosing that particular moment to voice her views because when you serve food or drink, you can safely take the stage.

She believes that all territories captured in the Six-Day War should be returned to their rightful owners, even at the expense of national security. She pours the coffee slowly into Daniella's cup. Daniella stops admiring her own art on the walls and actually listens to Rona, who says, "The left wing is crushed by the right wing in this country."

Rona herself feels crushed by her family and friends. She sets down the coffee pot and sits on the white sofa, opening herself to their verbal attacks.

"You want us to give up territories without a peace agreement?" Asher sounds amazed, although it isn't the first time he's hearing Rona's unpopular opinions.

"Look, the whole world is against us," Rona says. "We're considered occupiers, the new Nazis who inflict Holocaust upon others."

"The world loves the underdog." Asher sucks on his cigarette. "You'll get support only as a victim, which in our case means massacre in the streets of Tel Aviv. I'd rather be criticized."

"Asher, Asher, Asher." Rona sighs and cuts herself an extra-thin slice of chocolate cake, puts it on a small plate, then picks up a microscopic crumb on the tip of a tiny silver fork and tastes it daintily. Her eating is measured in the presence of others. When alone, her immense hunger overtakes her good manners and she doesn't bother with a plate or a fork.

"Those you approach in peace," Rona says, "respond in peace."

"Theoretically, you're right, but we aren't dealing with Switzerland here."

Rona says, "Tell me why." She takes another micro-bite of the cake.

"The Arabs aren't used to democracy. If you treat them the way you believe is fair, they get insulted and resent you. Look at all those Middle Eastern countries. Look at the facts. Is there any Arab country whose rulers treat its citizens fairly? They are all like Saddam, or Stalin, killing them and treating them like slaves, teaching their children to hate. They see your democracy as a weakness."

"You sound just like the Nazis," Rona says, calm, "when they spoke in generalities about the Jews."

"They won't rest." Asher raises his voice, starting to lose his temper. "They won't rest until the total obliteration—"

"Can you blame them?" Rona interrupts, her voice crackling with the question. "Maybe we don't belong here in the first place."

This is very simple for her. She knows they'll never understand.

"You shouldn't talk like this, after what happened to your mother's family." Eithan attacks from her far right. "If we hand over Tel Aviv and Jerusalem, we might as well give up the whole thing and open Auschwitz for business."

"Buchenwald," Rona corrects, cutting herself a second, this time hefty, slice of cake. "They starved to death in Buchenwald."

Daniella and Asher Schwartz agree with Eithan. They didn't always agree with him. Thirty-five years ago, Daniella the artist and her husband Dr. Asher were among those pseudofriends who had lynched him in absentia to save their own skin from the wrath of a damaged and hateful woman now dead of old age. Today they respect Eithan's opinions because he doesn't stutter anymore, he owns a successful software company that makes a fortune, his house is larger than theirs, and basketball is popular even among school teachers and parents.

Daniella refuses the cake. She stares at Rona with disapproval and says, "That slice alone is worth a thousand calories."

"Who cares?" Rona asks.

With Daniella you always had to listen to intake and uptake of calories, protein, and fat.

At two in the morning, Rona tires of their pointless arguments. She sits down at her Steinway and starts playing "The Moonlight Sonata." Her friends shut up and listen.

Rona's eyes are closed and the words of Beethoven's student whisper on her mind with the adagio. *A nocturnal scene, in which a mournful ghostly voice sounds from the distance.*

A ghost of a girl at an old piano is playing for a ghost of another girl who is listening, enthralled. Rona can feel Shelli behind her, a book in her lap, her eyes wide open into a daydream. Rona keeps playing. Now she is a woman and Shelli remains the little girl who lives through her music, the girl she had sacrificed for the acceptance of those now slumped behind her over fat sofas, half asleep, their energy spent. And the grown-up Rona, with her mournful, ghostly sonata, is telling the girl Shelli, *I used to play just for you.*

A cool gust of wind suddenly blows from the garden, a faucet has opened and Rona's eyes are dripping water. Still into the adagio, she allows herself a luxury error, just because Eva isn't here to yell out Hungarian insults at her. And Shelli isn't here, so why bother with perfection?

They keep talking while she plays, but Rona doesn't mind. She'd had enough piano-related attention by the age of twelve to last a lifetime.

Somewhere in the *Presto* she makes another intentional error, and this becomes a private joke between her new self and the child she used to be. Her ears ache. She wouldn't let her son get away with such slips. She feels rebellion and glee, as she had long ago desecrating her mother's home with Wagner.

When she's done playing, she swivels around. Her guests have left, the ashtrays are filled with dead cigarette butts, and Eithan is curled on the sofa with his shaggy dog, Max, both asleep. Max sleeps all day long lately, but how could Eithan? How anyone could sleep through that tempestuous presto agitato is beyond her.

Where is Shelli now? Rona wonders while clearing up.

8

A cookie jar illustrated with the forty-eight traditional Japanese sexual positions decorates the top of the piano, keeping Rona's favorite vanilla and chocolate cookies fresh at all times.

Gila, Rona's eighteen-year-old daughter, wants the jar for her own room. Fourteen-year-old Mike wants it for himself. Jihan avoids touching it when she dusts. Rona keeps moving the jar around, to a bookshelf, to the windowsill, to the old Erard. She was blessed with the Midas touch for aesthetics, a talent for presentation. The cookie jar ends up on the Steinway, where it poses like a priceless *objet d'art*.

"One position is missing here," Daniella whispers, goading.

"Meaning?" Rona's face burns. *Here we go again. Ancient history.*

"You should know." Daniella winks. Then she changes her tone. "It must have cost a fortune."

Rona allows Daniella to steer away from the dangerous subject of positions and answers with pride: "Twenty shekels in the flea market, but I brought it down to fifteen."

The Rosenthals are very well off financially, but Rona loves to bargain and to boast about it. She buys even her clothes in discount stores. All she really needs is a few loose cotton dresses. Those are comfortable, don't constrain her movements when she cooks or teaches piano lessons in the scorching Israeli summers. One resembles a pinkish-red sundress she wore nonstop in high school. Eithan used to slip his hand through it when they sat in a movie theater, in class or anywhere else. One day the dress disappeared, but it's just as well. It wouldn't fit her today. And it's been a long time since Eithan slipped his hand through anything she wore.

Rona teaches piano lessons not for the money, but out of pure love for both music and instruction.

She enjoys saving money. She would drive halfway across town to buy detergent for half the price, in the meantime doubling what she'd pay for gas. She doesn't see the irony. Rona isn't cheap, but economical. She doesn't go as far as Eva and her war mentality, Eva who used to lay aside her daily bath water for scrubbing the floors. The floors that gleamed.

Rona isn't as obsessed with floors as Eva. Hers are white marble with gold veins. She and Eithan imported the marble from Italy to match the Jerusalem stone in the bathrooms.

They have five bathrooms, one for each family member and one for a guest. Each bathroom has big mirrors, Eithan's idea. Rona—who sees more and more of Eva in herself—has grown to hate mirrors. They show every line and extra fold of skin and fat. She doesn't have real wrinkles yet, only the rolls of fat and a spare tire around her waist.

Rona's oldest daughter, Tally, a religious woman, looks away from the cookie jar when she visits. All those naked people in intricate poses are an abomination. Moishe, Tally's orthodox husband, can't help looking right at it. Rona catches him glancing at the jar frequently from the corner of his eye. If he were a Catholic, she believes he would cross himself.

She leaves the jar where it is. This is her home and the fanatics can squirm all they want while showing their hypocrisy.

Tally has twin boys, Eithan-Nathan and Mike-Meir, and a newborn baby girl, Roni-Rivka. Each child has a secular name and a Hebrew name. Tally allows her mother to watch the kids, as long as Rona keeps her promise not to teach them even one note of music until their bar mitzva.

"No music boot camp for my children," says Tally, who instead puts them through the boot camp of religion.

Rona has made the promise. The twins, three years old in July, are at the perfect age to start lessons as their fingers are supple and their brains clean slates.

When she still dared to argue about it, Rona had said, "If we wait until their bar mitzva, we may miss a great talent."

"Good. They'll have a normal life," Tally said, stubborn.

Rona has to walk on eggshells because of her firstborn's quick temper, so she lets Tally have her way.

Rona considers it unfair. The boys shouldn't be deprived of education just because Tally was traumatized by daily musical discipline. So far, Rona sticks to her word. When her grandsons stare longingly at the piano, she smiles down at them and says, "Later."

She waits until Eithan and the others are all gone, then she lets the kids sit at the baby grand and bang on the keys, which is really all they do. Every now and then Rona's hand guides them, but just a little, or she'll drop a word or two of instruction. The boys will open their eyes at her and listen with wonder. They are human sponges, absorbing her words the way her own children—Tally, Gila and even Mike—never had.

Little Eithan sometimes moves his entire tiny body when he "plays." This dance rhythm surprised and delighted Rona when she first saw it, but unlike other proud grandmas, she couldn't share the miracle with anyone in her unappreciative family. Each one of them would side with Tally against Rona.

Rona still has jurisdiction over her two younger children, Gila and Mike. She forces both to practice on alternate afternoons from four to six. When they refuse, she yells, but unlike Eva, she yells in Hebrew and mostly never in the presence of their friends. When they're done with the serious stuff, they play for fun. Sometimes all three of them sit in a row, Rona in the center (still the center) and they play that quick piece for six hands that Mike wrote. He's the real talent, but Rona makes Gila play because the fundamentals of music never hurt anyone.

Mike's ears are laced with rings. A tattoo on the back of his shaved neck says, *A'am Im Ha'Golan*, a right-wing slogan pledging to keep the Golan Heights as part of Israel. This message on her son's shaved scalp infuriates Rona, who finds herself a political minority in her own family.

When piano practice is over, Gila and Mike play basketball with their father, using the hoop above the garage door.

Rona, chewing the end of a chocolate bar she'd started that morning but had managed to put aside, calls from the kitchen window, "Mike's recital is next week. If he breaks a finger, Eithan, I'll break your balls."

"Don't worry about broken fingers," Eithan calls out. "We'll be careful."

An angle of the house conceals the hoop from the kitchen's window, and Rona can't see what's going on. She would die if she saw Mike's beautiful long fingers—those that just played a complex Scriabin prelude—spinning the ball high above his shaved head.

9

Eithan had hoped one of his kids would show interest in basketball. Tally married as soon as she legally could. Mike enjoys the game, uses basketball as a form of revolt against Rona, who's obsessed with the well-being of his hands.

Gila could be the one, if she'd only stop gaining weight. Whenever she scores a basket, which happens often, Gila smiles at her father and brushes her dark hair back with her fingertips. Eithan melts at that gesture. In it he can see his old girl, Rona, who used to toss her long braids over her shoulders.

How beautiful she used to be. Rona, his first and only love, had believed in him when the others, including his own mother, had considered him an idiot.

Rona had been the queen of the class. The boys, also the girls, adored her. Gidi Ishbitzky had been envious of him. And Asher Schwartz tried to steal Rona away on that camping trip to the Yehuda desert, even though he was already dating Daniella. The "boys," now pushing fifty, still hang out together, rehashing the ancient stories. They love to mention that day when they all walked in on Rona and that other girl.

Poor Rona was teased for years and that other girl . . .

"She'd read all the time," Asher says.

Gidi asks, "What was her name? Shiri? Shula?"

"Shelli," Eithan says. He always has to remind them.

"Yes," Asher says. "Remember how Rona dropped her?"

"Right." Eithan wishes they'd change the subject. All they know or care about is the shallow stuff, and they used to call *him* stupid—*that girl* liked to read; *the thing* happened, then

Rona dropped her. But Eithan had a soft spot for *that girl*, thought of her often. He'd known Shelli better than any of them. She'd been kind to him. She knew he'd been only playing stupid.

Rona was never a bully, but her powerful influence over her friends was strong. When she'd ceased all association with Shelli, that was automatically the end of Shelli's friendships with the rest of the clique, the hev're—Daniella, Asher, Eithan, Le'ora and Gidi.

The quiet Shelli had always been a fifth wheel anyway. Just about glued to Rona, having considered Rona her best friend. Yet for Rona, Shelli was only one of many. Or so it seemed to Eithan.

It had been the early seventies. Israel had its own problems, unrelated to Vietnam and Nixon, but American culture was a strong influence—the clothes, the music, that commune attitude. Rona's room was always packed with her girlfriends—a substitute for the large family she'd never had.

When Eithan joined them, he had to plow through tanned arms and legs just to be able to sit next to Rona. They used to drape themselves on every centimeter of that long, narrow space—on Rona's bed, on cushions, on the floor—and listen to the Platters, the Supremes, Simon and Garfunkel, Joan Baez and the Beatles. They used to change John Lennon's words to "Imagine there's no people, and wouldn't that be fine. People fuck up the planet..."

Rona and her girlfriends didn't mind his presence, treated him as one of them. Sometimes he'd come in and see the dimmed lights and the girls enjoying a little party, slow dancing with each other, giggling, practicing for Friday night's party, for the real thing they all cared about, dancing with the boys. He'd see Daniella dancing with Rona, Le'ora with Shelli, or Le'ora with Rona.

Rona and Shelli.

That particular union felt threatening somehow. He didn't know why at the beginning, but he eventually found out.

Shelli would get between him and Rona, which drove Eithan crazy. When the hev're left, Shelli would stay and get in their way of being alone. It was such a waste when Rona's parents were gone, along with Uri, Rona's snotty-nosed little brother. The apartment could have been his and Rona's, but Shelli never left.

Today Uri is one of Eithan's closest friends. When Uri was little, Eithan thought him repulsive with that thick green mucus constantly glued to the space between his nose and his upper lip. Uri's mother—now Eithan's mother-in-law—should have spared some of the floor-scrubbing time for her son's face.

Anyway, Shelli would take a book off the shelf and start reading next to them on the bed. How hot he was for Rona. His balls would hurt, but he was forced to compete with a girl.

"Why c-can't she read in her own h-home?" Eithan asked in a whisper.

"Her mother won't let her read these books," Rona explained, always defending Shelli.

"What k-kind of smut is she reading? Fa-Fanny Hill?"

"Ka-Tsetnik."

"Ka-ka-ka . . . what?"

Eithan couldn't understand why Rona let Shelli stay after everyone else left. Couldn't she go and read in the living room, by that piano she adored? Once, Eithan slid his hand across Rona's back, expecting to have a struggle with that tricky bra, but the clasp was already undone. Another hand, not his own, was there. He should have known then.

Then Asher Schwartz told Eithan what Daniella Levy had told him in confidence.

"Dani said that during one of those practice dances, Shelli kissed Rona. Well, all the girls practice kissing, but Shelli stuck her tongue into Rona's mouth and Rona *pretended* to like it. At least that's what Rona claimed when Dani and Le'ora asked her." Asher widened his eyes and added, "Gidi Ishbitzky told me that Le'ora told *him* that from her angle, Rona's acting wasn't acting at all. Rona's tongue wasn't exactly passive and her hand was, well, on Shelli's breast."

"What are you sa-saying, Asher?" Eithan asked, clenching his hand into a fist.

"You'd better ask your girlfriend if she *is* your girlfriend," Asher said.

Once again, Eithan bloodied Asher's nose. He didn't believe him and he was angry at him for spreading rumors about Rona. Of course he wasn't going to ask her such a question.

He didn't need to ask because the next day he and the hev're walked in on the real action.

Afterward, the gossip machine went into overdrive. The story was blown out of proportion, bigger than anything else going on in school. Bigger even than the recent story of Sarit Cohen having to get an abortion after being knocked up by Raffi, the sleazy gym teacher.

Rona swore to Eithan that it happened just that once, and that Shelli was the one who had talked her into it. Eithan was the perfect gentleman. The way he saw it, Rona had sheltered him in grade school only a few years before. It was his turn to stick by her and protect her from the more dangerous high school mob. He became Rona's rock, escorting her everywhere, waiting for her even outside the lavatories. He would steer Rona away from Shelli and her bad influence as well as from the cruel whispers of their so-called friends. Those friends who

A Small Country about to Vanish

—while moving on to the next piece of juicy gossip—actually didn't forget.

Eithan believed Rona's claim that it had been Shelli's fault, but the excuse seemed illogical. Rona was a natural leader. Why would she let Shelli, anyone, talk her into something she didn't really want? Since no one expected logical thoughts from Eithan, he kept the question to himself.

From then on, and just to prove her point, Rona stopped talking to Shelli.

All or nothing. That's the way Rona was and still is.

She used to be so beautiful and shapely. Now she's overweight, having completely let herself go. All or nothing. Why does she have to go to such extremes? Daniella used to be an ugly girl, too thin and with large rabbit's teeth and huge ears. When she married Asher, and many plastic surgeries later, she became the glamour queen of Tel Aviv's night scene.

Occasionally Asher digs at Eithan, "Now who's lucky?" Good-heartedly, of course, no malice.

Gila steals the ball from Mike, dribbles like a pro and scores again.

Eithan and Rona always protected each other. *Tristan und Isolde*. He'll never forget that day in grade school when the miserable Mrs. Schiller and the rest of them twisted the knife. *Delinquent. Aggressive. Slow. Doesn't comprehend the text.* Had he actually been in that classroom, listening to those insulting words, or had he made Rona's memories his own? After so many years together, their experiences intermingled.

Eithan hears the screeching of tires. Tally, in a stylish head wrap and a calf-long religious dress, emerges from her Mercedes Benz. She slams the car door, waves at the three of them by the garage, and without speaking, pushes the front door open. By the way she stomps in, Eithan knows he should stay out of it. Still, he hears her raised voice from inside the house.

10

"You promised," Tally yells.

"I kept my promise," Rona says, bewildered, as she irons Mike's white shirt for next week's recital. Way ahead of time, but this is a big deal and she needs to be ready.

"*Baruch hashem*, little Eithan speaks well for a three-year-old, but where would a boy his age learn the word *staccato*?"

"He could have heard his uncle say it." Rona blames big Mike as she presses his shirt's collar. Tally would never get angry at her brother, her confidante.

Apparently little Mike repeated the word *staccato* at home, the way kids frequently do while learning to speak. Tally has no sense of humor about it. She behaves as if Rona had taught the boy a dirty curse word in five languages.

Tally had always searched for her own set of spiritual rules. At first it was mild, yoga and meditation. When she turned fourteen she declared herself a Buddhist and set up a shrine in her bedroom with fat Buddha statues and prints of turquoise and gold. She would burn incense that gave her little sister sneezing fits. She ate nothing but raw fruits and vegetables. She became obsessed with her bodily functions, recording every scrap she put in her mouth and what came out the other end, including duration, odors and consistency.

Immediately following her military service, Tally found reiki. Then reiki was replaced by some other group whose name Rona didn't remember. "Woman who wear jeans have no self-respect," was one of her pearls of wisdom from that period.

Each time Tally had re-invented herself, she tried to convert everyone else, pontificating about yoga or reiki or vegetarianism being the right way. It was the same with her boyfriends. Each time she fell in love, the boyfriend's philosophy became the word of wisdom everyone had to follow.

Moishe and his God would become her ultimate self-realization. When she married Moishe, she started wearing, along with a stylish head cover, a beatific look of serenity on her face. That serenity, however, was fragile. Rather than becoming calmer by her *hazara be'tshuva*, Tally became angrier and often lost her temper.

"You're teaching them music," Tally accuses. "What next, *im yirze hashem*? *Legato*? *Legatissimo*? 'The Moonlight Sonata' beginning to end by the age of four, *shenizke le'haim arukim*?"

Baruch hashem. Im yirze hashem. All those compulsive blessings and bargainings with an imaginary presence. Rona cringes at the fake expressions of faith woven into her daughter's yelling. A crease on the sleeve she's ironing doesn't want to go away.

Rona says, "When little Eithan plays 'The Moonlight Sonata' beginning to end, it'll be his form of rebellion."

"Why would he need rebellion?"

"The way of nature." Rona spritzes a thin spray on the white shirt. "Your son will become a secular piano composer, jazz, just to spite you. You use religion against me. I used Wagner against my mother."

"*Tfu.*" Tally makes the sound of spitting without actually bothering to spit. "Wagner, that Nazi swine—"

"Think about Nazi swine when you get into your new Mercedes," Rona says.

"Don't change the subject," Tally says. "One more musical word out of either of my sons' mouths and you'll never see them again."

"Isn't *honor thy father and mother* something you should consider in your sudden piety?" Rona asks.

She immediately regrets her words. Tally has the power to rob her of the sweetness of her grandchildren. Rona stops ironing, puts her beautiful hands with the long, thin fingers on her chest and promises, "No mention of music until the boys are bar mitzva, and even then only when they can sing their *haftarah* by heart."

Tally storms out of the house just as she had stormed into it ten minutes earlier. Rona is convinced Tally married Moishe just to annoy her secular parents. Why else was she attracted to him? She was becoming as fanatical about religion as her charmless husband.

*

Gila scores another basket and says, "Got to go."

She sees the relief in Eithan and Mike's faces. Gila is taller than both of them, and she kicks their butts every time.

She showers, puts on her jeans and leather jacket and last, that orange lipstick she borrowed from Sophie. She notices how it changes the color of her eyes from hazel to light green. As she steals a last glance in the mirror, she makes sure to cover her forehead with her bangs. If only this acne would go away, she'd be pretty. Gila gets into her blue Fiat—her parents' gift for her big birthday—and rushes to Avivim to meet Sophie and Ramón.

Ramón is gorgeous, almost as tall as Gila, and his crooked nose adds sex appeal to his Latin/Jewish features. His Argentinian accent drives Gila crazy. The athletic Sophie is covered with tattoos and rings. Wind surfing is her thing. Both Sophie and Ramón have a crush on Gila, but Ramón has a better chance since Gila, so far, believes herself straight.

Ice cream cones in their hands, they wander the mall and discuss the latest pigua, in Netanya, in which so many died.

Sophie teases Ramón. "Don't you read the newspapers in Buenos Aires? A fine time for your family to immigrate to this *nekuda mezuyenet,* this little fucked-up spot on the globe."

Ramón says *mezuyenet* a few times, practicing the new word.

Gila loves his reserved, foreign style, so unlike the loud and outgoing sabres of his age group, yet he is popular in school and his sense of irony and nuance transcends his language barrier. She adores the uncertain way he pronounces new Hebrew words and gets the meaning distorted. Mezuyenet, for instance, can mean fucked-up or excellent, depending on the pronunciation of the *Z* sound.

When Ramón gets a word wrong, he seems so vulnerable. His dark eyes fill with humor and at the same time with sadness and longing for his own language and his faraway homeland.

"Fucked-up," he says, "but with some future, some choices."

Gila says, "You can't even choose between being shot and getting blown up."

"At least I'll die with my stomach full of ice cream," Ramón says. He kisses Gila. "And with the most beautiful girl beside me."

Sophie, an out-of-the-closet lesbian, pokes her tongue at him midlick and wiggles it, showing off a gold ring.

"Is it true what they say about the ring?" Gila asks.

Sophie grins. "None of my girlfriends has complained so far. Want a ride?"

A Small Country about to Vanish

"Tempting." Gila laughs.
Ramón asks, "Can I watch?"

*

After another hour of basketball with his dad, a sweaty Mike takes a shower and gets ready to meet his friends—shaved heads, tattoos, all-over piercings, different and uniform at the same time. They shave and pierce and tattoo to set themselves apart from their parents who grew up in the wild sixties and seventies but are now considered total establishment.

Mike will meet his friends at the Avivim shopping mall for falafel and a few rounds of bowling. When he is one foot out the door, both his parents warn, "Be careful," knowing very well the warning is an empty one. It can happen anywhere, anytime.

A disgruntled boy from the Palestinian side—exactly Mike's age—can blow himself up in a crowd of shoppers. If this is Mike's unlucky day, the X-ray of his lungs will look like a white butterfly and the doctors at the emergency room will say, "Nothing we can do."

If he is lucky to be far away enough from the explosion, he may only lose his index finger and close all arguments between his parents about his future in either music or basketball. Rona will say, "Thank God you're alive, fuck the finger."

Secretly, however, she'd mourn the loss of her son's career. So would Eithan. All their hopes rest on Mike and Gila.

11

Rona knows she shouldn't and yet does it anyway. On a routine check for drugs in Gila's room, she discovers a package of birth control pills in one of the desk drawers. She waits for Gila to come home from school and right there, in Gila's room, she hands her the package, a question in her eyes.

Gila snatches the package. "If you snoop, you deserve to find out."

"How did you get a prescription?" Rona asks.

"Dr. Rosenblatt," Gila says.

"Daniella's doctor?"

"Uh-huh." A hint of a vicious smile touches Gila's lips.

Rona is beyond hurt at this double betrayal. Her best friend and her daughter formed a union without her. "Why didn't you come to me?"

"Because I didn't," Gila says.

"I hope you also use condoms," Rona says.

"Why would you care if I live or die?" Gila's voice carries a magnitude of venom Rona hasn't heard before. "You only care about that stupid piano."

Gila's accusation resonates, striking an old chord, one of Rona's repressed memories she's never dealt with. Many years ago she'd opened the door to her own childhood room, her little sanctuary with the posters of the Beatles, the macramé and the colorful cushions on which she and her friends sat and straightened their hair in a long process called *abu ageila*. They had celebrated their own mini Woodstock festival only the day before. But on that day she caught Eva sitting on her bed, something resting in her lap. *Wagner. She's found my Wagner*, Rona cried out inside.

But it had been worse than Wagner.

Rona's diary was open in Eva's lap, and Eva was rocking back and forth, silently crying. Eva never cried, or, for that matter, did anything silently.

"What did you read?" Rona had asked, more angry than concerned.

"I could take the Nazis," Eva said, pushing herself up with some difficulty into a standing position. "But this, from you?"

Rona still has that diary. Moisture had glued those two pages together and she can't, won't, pry them open. Some memories are better left unremembered. What she does recall is the cruelty of her spoken words, as if the written ones hadn't caused enough pain.

"I see," Rona had said, "that your Hebrew is good enough to read what you shouldn't."

Why had her mother gone there in the first place? And why had she, Rona, invaded Gila's territory? She wasn't looking for drugs, but rather for secrets Gila was keeping from her. And she'd found both drugs and secrets.

"*Sliha*," Rona says, the ambiguous Hebrew word that could mean *get out of my way* but in this particular context means *forgive me*.

As she had never apologized to her mother, Rona now apologizes to her daughter for her own intrusion. She leaves Gila's room—ten times larger than her own childhood sanctuary, and decorated lavishly in lavender and blues, not a macramé shade in sight—knowing this will be forever Gila's private moment of maternal betrayal, a landmark in her young life. A touchstone for the future.

12

Rona parks her car by Avivim, the popular shopping center. Mike's recital is tomorrow and she is hoping to find a new dress. As she glides up the external escalator, Tel Aviv slowly reveals itself beneath her feet in its rich colors. As always, she's overwhelmed by the city's density, the mix of old and new. Gray apartment buildings from the turn of the twentieth century, tarnished by dust and neglect, their rooftops covered with ugly solar heaters, are buried deep among new high-rises just as ugly in Rona's eyes.

The sight of apartment buildings, old or new, gives her claustrophobia. She grew up in one of those—it was already old back then—fourth floor, third apartment on the left. The mixed smells of ethnic cooking and disinfectant hit her memory receptors when she thinks of running down the dark stairwell, skipping three stairs at a time, always in a hurry to get away from home, out to the street to meet her friends.

Rona sees the laundry hanging outside small balconies and thinks of Eva leaning over the window, fastening wet garments to a long line where they would dry all day in the hot sun. Rona's clothes and bed sheets had always smelled of sunshine. Eva, now in her eighties, doesn't scrub floors anymore, yet she still dries the laundry in the sun as she doesn't believe in dryers.

Rona and Eithan have a room ready for Eva, who refuses to move in with them although she can barely climb all those stairs. "I've moved enough times in my life," she says, still in Hungarian.

A Small Country about to Vanish

When Rona visits her mother, she grabs on to the balustrade, huffs and puffs and stops frequently to catch her breath. She is out of shape, fat and almost fifty.

The mall, unlike the old apartments, makes it easy on their customers. The escalator is purposely slow, allowing a gradual, spreading view of a busy Tel Aviv afternoon to unfold before the shoppers.

Rona isn't enchanted. Too much traffic, too many cars, too many people hurrying around her and too much movement, with children jumping and playing on the stairs.

So many spicy ingredients are mixed together in this pressure cooker, no wonder the mix occasionally explodes. She can hear those small explosions in the form of laughter, loud talking, Middle Eastern music blasting from car windows.

This country wants to be heard, and in the process it annoys the world Rona loves to travel. Those with financial means travel abroad as a form of escape. Rona and Eithan get out of the pressure cooker as frequently as possible. Unfortunately, there are diplomatic limitations for those holding an Israeli passport, leaving some countries out of their reach.

The views and sounds of her city bring tears of love and doubt to Rona's eyes. Does she have a right to this love, or is she loving stolen property?

Tel Aviv did not exist. She can almost hear Eithan's argument. Someone always argues with her about something, anything. *Tel Aviv was nothing but sand until the Jews took over.*

She hears a harsh, discordant mixture of imaginary voices —her friends, her children, the whole population of her beleaguered Israel—telling her, *This is your homeland to love or hate. You can travel the world, but there's only one home for you.*

The doubts of her belonging gnaw in Rona's stomach, making her hungry. Lately everything makes her hungry. She pictures a Greek salad and a huge grilled cheese sandwich smothered with Kalamata olives. That's what she'll order at Café International.

She watches the approach of a matronly middle-aged woman, pleasantly plump, in a midcalf-length black Armani dress. *Dignified*, Rona thinks, *but she looks like my mother*. Then she realizes she's studying her own reflection in the mirrored sliding doors. Since Rona avoids mirrors, any sighting of her body is a surprise. Her mental picture of herself is very different from reality. In her head she's slim and feminine, with Tiger Lily braids, as she was years ago.

Avivim in its elegance is not unlike the Beverly Center in Los Angeles, and Rona constantly compares the two. She sees the same stores and restaurants she's seen all over the world. The major differences are the rich assortment of spoken languages. Hebrew prevails, but it is mixed with Russian and Arabic sounds, Spanish and guttural Moroccan French.

The guard runs a metal detector over her body, sticks his face into her blue purse and pleasantly says, "Have a safe evening."

Safe, not *nice*.

A group of female soldiers, girls, really—soon her Gila will be one of them—are wearing short-skirted army fatigues, their long legs tanned and toned. They're giggling and licking ice cream. Submachine guns are slung from their shoulders, looking very natural, in the same way Rona carries her Vuitton purse. But this is abnormal. Rona is suddenly alien to this shocking scene. Those loaded magazines in their belts are wrong and crazy to the bone.

Many years ago Rona was one of them in a miniskirt, balancing a heavy Uzi on her shoulder and an ice cream cone in her hand. Pink strawberry ice-cream to match her pink nail polish. She'd sit at her Singer sewing machine with Le'ora and Daniella, taking up the hem of their khaki skirts to the highest allowable measurement.

She'd had to learn to avoid an accidental discharge of her Uzi. The sight of these girls carrying deadly weapons so casually, combined with the fact that such a sight is taken for granted by everyone, is a definite sign of national insanity.

Rona meets her girlfriends every other afternoon. Sometimes five of them get together, relaxing with their coffee while their children are at dance/rollerblades/music/basketball lessons. The husbands occasionally join them.

Today only Daniella is waiting for her. The two have been friends ever since Eithan and Asher chased them around the schoolyard and pulled on their braids.

They order their usuals. Daniella gets café *botz*, mud coffee, so titled for the layer of black deposits at the bottom. If you need extra caffeine, you chew those grains and you'll stay up all night and eventually get an ulcer. As for Rona, her family and current events are enough to give her that ulcer. She likes her coffee less harsh—cappuccino with extra milk and whipped cream on top. The shapely Daniella reminds Rona of her skinnier days.

She decides against the full meal and orders a cheese pastry, hoping Daniella will split it with her, knowing full well she'll eat it all herself. You don't throw away leftovers when so many children are starving. Now, this doesn't happen in prosperous Israel, but still, starvation exists in the world.

"I didn't eat anything since breakfast," Rona says, justifying her bottomless hunger.

Daniella's smallness makes Rona feel big and awkward, although thirty kilos overweight is totally normal for a woman in her late forties who had three children. It may be more like thirty-five kilos lately, but still, normal.

A sexy blonde in a tight black dress sashays by their table, cleavage down to here, legs up to there. Her lips are bright red, as if she's just bitten into a juicy fruit.

Rona stops chewing long enough to say, "Bloodsuckers, those Russian women."

"I don't know about blood." Daniella sips her café botz, leaving a red lipstick mark on the fat mug.

"Look at her," Rona says. "She's about our age. Swaying her hips and the men are drooling."

"And what's wrong with that?"

"They come to our country and steal our men."

"I can't believe that came out of your mouth," Daniella says, now annoyed. "You don't even feel entitled to this country, yet suddenly this is *our country* and *our men*. Who can steal a grown man?"

The Russian woman slowly sways her pelvis as she walks. Rona can imagine her nakedness through the dress. She averts her gaze, only to realize that others—her fellow diners, men and women at small tables outside the packed café—have stopped whatever they were doing—talking, eating—just to stare.

"She has an eye magnet in her ass." Daniella laughs. "And I agree, there is something about Russian women. Either it's the language or the mannerisms. Yesterday I was looking for shampoo at the drugstore and this shopping consultant asked if she could help me in a heavy Russian accent. She wasn't particularly beautiful, but there was something so sexy about her, I wanted to ask when and where."

"I didn't know you had it in you," Rona says.

Daniella darts a look at Rona, one that hits its mark center bull's-eye, *We know you used to have it in you. We all remember*.

"This is a prelude to a suicide bomb," Rona says. "No one is paying attention. I guess she'd be considered a collaborator."

"Don't be ridiculous, Rona. What's your problem today?"

"Gila is . . ."

That whole business of the birth control pills is her problem, as is the alliance—no, the conspiracy—the two of them formed against her. That's the way Rona sees it. A conspiracy. She wants to confront Daniella.

"Gila, is . . . Well, even my Gila doesn't dress like this."

True. Her pretty Gila hides in her clothes.

*

At that moment, Gila and three of her girlfriends are trying on dresses at Free Spirit Boutique, a few stores south of Café International. All of them are eighteen, about to graduate from high school and enlist in the military, all happy to be alive. They're wearing shiny scarves they just bought, different colors but a similar style.

A blond woman studies the merchandise in the window.

"This chick looks like Anna K." Sophie's skin glows with that green scarf tied around her head. When they look at her quizzically, she explains, "You know, the tennis star who never won tournaments but dazzled the crowds with her beauty."

"A lesbian would know this," Lorena says, teasing.

Lorena also knows tennis. She used to play in her native Russia. Her mother still tries to coach her, but soccer and basketball, not tennis, are the national crazes in Israel nowadays.

Anna K.'s dead ringer walks in and Miri, the shop owner, is all over her with greetings.

Gila knows she's Russian because of those Slavic cheekbones, the tiny nose, the fair coloring and that extra pound of make-up. Then the woman opens her mouth and asks, her Hebrew gooey with Russian undertones, "May I try this red one, please?"

She's beautiful. Not a spot on her forehead, not an ounce of fat on her frame.

I wish I had her face, Gila thinks. And her figure.

Gila already shows the alarming signs of being overweight. Not really fat, but she'll always have to watch her diet. When she catches a glimpse of herself in the mirror, she sees Rona and she hates what she sees. *What possessed me to wear this?*

Gila's first dream is to get rid of the nasty acne. Her other dream is to have gorgeous legs like her mother's. She only wears shorts for basketball practice, and even then she isn't happy about it. Aba's obstacle to basketball glory was disapproval of the system; Gila's obstacle is heredity. She has Ima's figure. She's inherited Rona's heavy midsection and skinny fingers when it should have been the other way around. She wishes Rona had given her those great legs instead. She knows it isn't her mother's fault; nevertheless, she feels resentment because her mother always gets things wrong and this is just another wrong thing.

Now the resentment is compounded by that whole incident of the birth control pills. Rona apologized for trespassing, but Gila already decided to milk her mother's guilt for all it's worth. She won't talk to her for a few days, just to stress the importance of her privacy.

Only recently Gila had given Rona the silent treatment for another matter, that trip to Poland.

Gila and some of her best friends were handpicked by Mr. Goldman, the handsome history teacher, to accompany him on a field trip to Auschwitz. Gila was so excited about it, so looking forward to traveling. Maybe she wanted to go for the wrong reasons, but so what?

She'd been madly in love with Mr. Goldman for months, and she'd imagined scenarios in which they'd have a serious conversation and he'd discover her brilliance, maybe hold her hand. That's all she dared fantasizing, one-on-one conversations with Mr. Goldman. Okay, in one of the fantasies she and Mr. Goldman were left alone in a gas chamber, about to be gassed by the Nazis, and in the last moments of her life, he kissed her and said, My love for you will never die.

Her plans were ruined by Rona, who has all these hang-ups no one gives a shit about anymore. She has to be different, has to stick to archaic, crazy ideas even though she knows she'll ruin her daughter's life.

Mr. Goldman came to the house to talk to Gila's parents—Gila nearly fainted when she saw him at the door. Her father had no problem with letting her go, but Rona had to consider some deep principles and, no matter what, she wouldn't listen to reason. Gila could've died of shame when her mother started giving him crap.

She can still hear Rona's exact words.

"We have no business returning to the scene of the crime, Mr. Goldman. The murderers should go there, not us."

That was the end of the conversation. Gila waited for him to leave, then she barraged her mother with painful words, words designed to hurt going in and then again when replayed in the silence of night.

"You're just like Grandma. You're even starting to look like her. I wish Daniella were my mother."

Sophie clings to her, pulling her from her memories. "Gila, look."

The Russian carries a few dresses into one of the stalls and the girls linger to see what she'll look like when she comes out. This particular store doesn't have mirrors inside the fitting rooms. A business gimmick, forcing the costumer to come out in the clothes she's trying on. Then Miri, the shop owner, makes a big fuss, saying, "The pink is great on you," even if that shade gives your cheeks the pasty-dead tinge of kidney failure.

Miri doesn't have to lie to the Russian woman. That red little dress fits her perfectly. To Gila's surprise, the woman stares at her own reflection, screws up her face and goes back into the fitting room. She tries on a few more outfits and looks amazing in all of them, like a model on the runway. The flimsy, shimmering dress with the thin straps makes Lorena gawk and whisper, "I'm going to die now."

The Russian puts the red one back on, scrunches her own black dress into a little ball and sticks it into her purse. She pays Miri in cash. On her way out she stops at one of the mirrors and renews her very red lipstick. She notices the girls staring at her and smiles at Gila.

Gila doesn't smile back. "Shit," she says. "I almost forgot basketball."

*

Basketball practice, piano practice, practice, practice, practice. *Ima and Aba keep us constantly busy*, Mike thinks, not really pondering why. He's at the video arcade in Avivim with his friend Amos. A joystick in his hand, he stares down at his Spiderman watch. It's almost four. Time to go home and work on that Scriabin piece for tomorrow's recital.

As he and Amos descend the stairs on their way out, they pass a hot-looking blonde in a red dress ascending the same stairs with a purpose. Mike's fourteen-year-old body immediately tightens in response.

"Going camping?" Amos asks with a smile.

"What?" Mike instinctively looks down.

The thing in his pants with the mind of its own had made a little tent. Mike rushes home, hoping to find himself alone for just a few minutes. Before hitting the Steinway, he locks his bedroom door and takes care of the tent.

*

The Red Dragon is a popular restaurant on the second floor of the Avivim shopping center. Eithan Rosenthal, who left his office early, is waiting patiently for Marina, a cup of Chinese tea cooling in front of him. The place is dark. A seated customer can see who comes in, but the eyes of those entering take a few minutes to adjust.

In his need to justify his secret actions, Eithan has become a philosopher. What are we all doing at a shopping mall, he wonders. Why are we turning ourselves into targets? It has to do with the promise of a thrill. We're attracted to Avivim for the reason we're attracted to bungee jumping, skiing down a wall in Switzerland, skydiving. Danger is thrilling and life is short, so let's make it sweet.

According to Eithan, the state of Israel is populated with horny men, their frigid wives, and Russian immigrant women who love to fuck. Therefore this dangerous habit of gathering into vulnerable clusters of humanity makes complete sense.

Anthropologically speaking, he concludes, suicide bombers changed the sex lives of Israelis. So did Mother Russia. For instance, take the early immigrants in the Galilee, boys and girls full of excitement who read poems by Pushkin and Pasternak and made love in haystacks. Nothing has changed since 1922.

And the promise is fulfilled for Eithan.

Marina enters, wearing a red dress. She's supposed to be inconspicuous, but all eyes are on her. Eithan feels the danger of being discovered, but also tremendous pride. *She's here for me. You are all dying, but in a few minutes I'll be the happiest man on earth.* He doesn't wait for her eyes to adjust. They have a secret code. He gets up and goes to the ladies room, first stall on the right.

A few minutes later, not a word spoken, his ass is pressed against a cold surface and when he looks down he sees a white toilet on the right, the door on the left and directly below, the center part of smooth golden hair, a luxurious cleavage and his own engorgement.

He groans in pleasure. "Aleksander Pushkin, you are God."

"Why Pushkin?" Marina asks because she, a late immigrant, has no reason to know about the interests of the early ones.

"He was big here in the twenties," Eithan says.

"No bigger than you."

Marina kisses the tip of his erect penis. Her blue eyes are full of mock innocence, looking up at him in question. Is it good? She opens her mouth wide and swallows him deep. A light suction, then release. Her cool hand cups his balls, long nails digging into his ass. He'll die if she ever stops. Lipstick drags like trails of blood on his penis as she pulls it out slowly. He's a big man, bigger than Pushkin and Pasternak put together.

Hell, why would they be put together?

The door in the next stall opens and someone uses the toilet. He hears the sounds of urinating, but he cares about only one thing. He keeps quiet and so does Marina. He tries to stay focused, blocking out the horrible noises, the distracting smells. The moment is almost ruined for him, but Marina saves it. She pulls up the hem of her red dress and starts touching herself. Her years of being a gymnastics champion pay off, and Eithan feels great love for communism and *perestroika*. Marina can balance on her toes and take care of him and herself at the same time. Viva Stalin. He groans again. The Russians should rule the country, the universe.

This is what he likes. His wife won't do it for him, but Marina gives a whole new meaning to that beaten-up, ancient expression about the land devouring its inhabitants.

Rona did it a few times when they first started experimenting . . . He shouldn't think about Rona now. At the most crucial moment, she acted with such disgust that he didn't want it from her anymore. Marina is a goddess. No need to clean himself up, because not a drop dripped and he didn't have to lift a finger. Her fingers did the work for both of them.

And before Marina, the cross-eyed Svetlana with the golden lateral incisor who was so hungry for his sperm, she would finish him off and start all over again. "This is a delicacy," Svetlana would say, her golden tooth gleaming brightly, like a star in the night's sky. "Better than vodka." And she loved her cheap vodka.

Svetlana was too much even for him, but Marina, the perfect woman, knows when the party is over.

When he explodes, he doesn't care if the world explodes with him and he becomes an item on the evening news. He can see the headlines: *forty killed, two hundred injured in a pigua that rocked the Avivim shopping mall in Tel Aviv*. If this happens, he knows his life has been lived to the fullest.

Exhaustion overcomes him and he wants to be left alone. Marina has to go to her husband, Alexei, who'll hang both of them upside down like sausages if he ever finds out.

Alexei is the worst thing about her, but also the best. Marina makes no demands. She allows Eithan to go back to his family and live a square, predictable life for the rest of the evening. He'll never divorce Rona, the love of his life. The mysteries are long gone and the magic is buried in extra fat, but the love is there.

He'll buy Rona some chocolate or red roses on the way out.

"Tomorrow at the Mexican place," he says.

"*Do svidaniya*," Marina whispers, and her voice turns him on again. There's no time for a quickie. The family is expecting him for dinner.

Part Two
TRISTAN

A Small Country about to Vanish

13

Eithan hands Rona two dozen red roses and kisses her cheek. She eyes him with suspicion as she carefully cuts the stems under water and arranges the roses in a clear vase. The table is set with dinner—a large salad, various dairy products and Jaffa oranges. Old Max wakes up for long enough to greet his master with a tired tail wag, then fall back asleep under the table. Gila and Mike are picking at the food, giving him wide smiles. They start to eat and, as usual, they discuss politics.

Gila can barely look at Rona, who tries to be conciliatory with, "Would you like some herb tea?" and "How was your day?"

Eithan can tell mother is on the losing side of another confrontation with her daughter.

The last blowout between the two took a whole month to clear up. Rona had refused to sign a consent allowing Gila to go on a class field trip. Eithan couldn't see the big deal about it. "Why not let the girl go with her friends?" he asked. "She's at this age of peer pressure and the need to belong."

Rona wouldn't even listen to their counterarguments. Afterward Gila had given her mother the silent treatment until it became inconvenient and she needed something from her.

Yes, Rona can be stubborn about the oddest things; still, she doesn't deserve to be treated that way. He'll have a word with Gila later.

"Another pigua," Rona tells them, crunching a carrot.

Eithan turns on the TV to watch the evening news.

"A suicide bomber detonated himself at six fifty p.m. in the central shopping center in Petah Tikva, east of Tel Aviv. The explosion happened outside, in front of an ice cream shop and a popular pizzeria, killing two. Twenty-seven people are wounded, eight seriously. One of the dead is an infant. The other is her grandmother."

*

Rona feels the scream gathering in her throat, suffocating her. They watch the gruesome images on television, dead bodies, partial bodies and a full, frontal view of the baby's head. It could be a profile, but with so much blood, it's hard to tell.

Calmly Rona suggests, "Let's watch the stupidest American movie."

For a change, they all agree with her.

Mike chooses a high school comedy full of cheerleaders, baseball and overly sexed boys and girls. They've watched that film so many times, they can recite the dialogue, but it still makes them laugh hysterically.

One of the funny lines causes Mike to spew soda out of his nose. Gila—stretched out on the carpet at Eithan's feet—completely loses it at the sight of her little brother coughing, dark Coke dripping from his mouth and nose.

Like blood, Rona thinks, her laughter suddenly frozen. Stress translates into a craving for comfort food.

"Ice cream, anyone?" she asks.

"No, thanks," they say in unison.

When she digs her silver spoon into chocolate and vanilla, Rona becomes the twenty-five percent minority again.

*

A Small Country about to Vanish

Later, in the huge bedroom—with bay windows overlooking the garden and the olive trees—Eithan takes off his pants. Since it's dark outside and the garden is invisible, he has no choice but to look at Rona naked. In the lamplight, he compares her full figure—her sagging breasts and stomach, those stretch marks, all of which she hides so well in clothes—with the memory of Marina's athletic slimness. Marina has two children, but she isn't fat.

Rona still has, always had, great legs.

He sees Rona glancing in the general direction of his crotch, then he sees the change in her expression. Rona could never hide her emotions.

"Did you stop anywhere on the way home?" she asks.

"Avivim," he says. "I stopped for roses."

He thinks it better to confess something, in case one of Rona's friends had seen him there. His own friends would know better than to blab.

"Avivim?" Rona asks with a touch of alarm she tries to control. "A lot of security hassle for just roses. Why didn't you stop at the flower stand outside the mall?"

He doesn't answer, thinking, *Why can't she leave me alone?*

Rona sees in her mind's eyes a fleeting image of the sleazy Russian with the pelvic sway. Eithan sees the same vision. They don't know it, but for a second, husband and wife are closer in their thoughts than they have been for months.

They lie on the king-size bed, kiss good night and turn their backs on each other.

Of course he gets it on the side. All his hev're do, so why shouldn't he?

Marina needs him as much as he needs her, no more, no less, so what's the harm? Just thinking about Marina's hunger, he feels an erection starting in the dark, Rona's fat body next to him.

She had seen the drag of lipstick, then she asked that question, as if she already knew. He loves Rona, but she doesn't turn him on anymore. What other choice does he have?

Once late at night, Eithan—Marina next to him—had driven deep into a field of alfalfa. His cellphone played the Bach melody—Rona, calling to find out if her husband was still alive. He was more alive than ever when he said, "I'm stuck in this incredible traffic."

He'd been stuck all right, between Marina's incredible legs.

"There's a bomb scare on the Haifa/Tel Aviv autostrada. The traffic jam is from here to the moon. No, don't worry, *motek*. Nothing is going to explode." He lied, exploding into Marina that very moment.

He always calls Rona motek, sweetie. He does love her.

All of Eithan's friends have mistresses, and those who don't, invent them to save face. They all love to start a story with "My Russian." For instance, Gidi told them, "My Russian girlfriend has such long legs, we sit at a restaurant and she plays with my balls under the table."

Why do Israeli men suffer from premature ejaculation, goes the old joke. *They can't wait to run and tell their hev're.*

Rona's brother, Uri, sometimes hangs out with the boys—all of them close to fifty, but still boys. Whenever Uri brags about his Anastasia, Eithan remains silent. Once, around the time of Svetlana, Eithan opened his mouth to tell a "my Russian" story, when he realized he was talking to his brother-in-law. He bit his tongue and took another drag of his cigarette. Uri would have shrugged it off, but Eithan has some decency.

What about the wives? They look the other way and take the children out for ice cream. The wives carry on as usual for the kids' sakes, for their aging parents, for financial reasons. They pretend not to know, but they hate Russian women. Some take their own lovers, but not Rona. She plays the piano and eats cookies while Eithan keeps fit shooting hoops with Mike and Gila.

Marina's husband, Alexei, is a big Russian mafia guy. If he finds out about her affairs, she'll be murdered in her sleep and Eithan will lose his arms, legs and dick.

All those teachers were right about sports making one stupid. Eithan has improved in math since giving up competitive basketball, so he knows that statistics give him more of a chance of being killed by Alexei than in a pigua.

Statistically, Israeli women and children die by suicide bombers while buying ice cream. The men get killed on the battlefield or at the hand of an Alexei. This thought serves as closure, a solution for his dilemma. Eithan falls asleep.

*

Eithan is snoring, but Rona can't sleep. He turns to face her, and his warm, sleeping breath is on her neck. His hair reeks of that sweet perfume again. She has lost him, she knows. Their bedroom is the dead zone.

Rona is haunted by the image of an eighteen-month-old baby girl with half her head blown off. A young woman, about Tally's age, wanted something sweet before dinner, and for that, tomorrow she'll bury both her mother and her baby daughter. Which one of them does she mourn the most?

Which one of us would you mourn, Tally?

Four o'clock in the morning and still Rona can't sleep. The split head stays with her. Her field of vision is also split, half-light, half-dark, and she's leaning toward the darkness. When she closes her eyes—still wide awake—she sees the split, and the dark part is growing, spreading like spilled blood. A migraine will come next.

What's left of my life? she wonders. Even my loving son is embarrassed by me.

Unlike Gila, Mike is sensitive, and his shame is subtle, yet she knows it by the way he acts around his friends. That slight decline of his shaved, tattooed head when she nags him about piano practice. She sees more of Eva in herself every day and, though she loves her mother, she hates the similarities.

Gila had hissed at her yesterday when Rona dangled the package of Estrostep between two fingers. Gila hates her. Tally married and escaped into religious fanaticism to spite her. The kids are closer to Eithan and all are allied against Rona, even in their politics. Especially in their politics. They want security and revenge while Rona wants fairness and equality.

The darkness grows, the room is airless. Rona gets up and opens the window. It doesn't help. The suffocation is coming from within herself. They'd all be better off if she were dead, she thinks.

She loves ice cream. All she has to do is choose the right place, the right time.

14

Rona Rosenthal stares into her cappuccino. Bubbles of white foam keep popping all over the surface of her cup, small explosions across a wide terrain of whipped cream. Having once smoked pot, she knows the astounding visual effects pot can create out of mundane objects. Pot is the answer, the sudden thought comes to her.

Call the media, the military. Pot is the only solution for peace in the Middle East. Let all the leaders smoke hashish. It'll make their food taste better, their sex will improve, their ability to remember will decline, and that'll be the end of wars and persecution. All the animosities of the Middle East, of the world, would be forgotten if people, all people of all nations, inhaled amnesia-generating chemicals. They'd sit in Ramallah, Gaza and East Jerusalem, smoke, eat and forget why they should hate the Jews. And the Jews would forget the pogroms, the *shaheed*s blowing themselves up, the Holocaust.

Calm down and eat, Rona tells herself. Good ideas won't solve anything in this absurd world. Pot or not, she's hungry now. So hungry, she can't wait for Daniella.

Rona polishes off the cinnamon pastry without even tasting its flavor. She'll have to supplement it with something more nutritious. When the waitress comes to the table, Rona orders her favorite grilled cheese sandwich. It comes with a lot of greens, so it isn't pure cholesterol.

At the next table a man is on the phone, asking if everything is okay. "*Ha'kol be'seder?*"

Another pigua happened today, this time at a shish kabob restaurant in Haifa. Even without knowing the man, Rona knows that he's going down the list of his loved ones, verifying that everyone is alive.

When a bomb goes off somewhere, Rona does a mental count of everyone she knows who may have been there. Their numbers are programmed on her cellphone. She'd ask that same one question, no more. She's already done her daily calling queue. The authorities kindly request that citizens not overload the system with long conversations during an emergency.

A sandwich arrives. Too large, with too much surrounding salad.

The man at the next table keeps dialing and asking, "Ha'kol be'seder?"

All his earthly cares have narrowed to one smaller than Rona's sandwich. When he gets through the list, he may drink up his coffee in one gulp, down to the mud at the bottom, and go to a secret meeting place to have his daily quickie with his Russian girlfriend. Afterward, he may pop into the nearest flower shop and buy red roses for a wife who doesn't provide blow jobs.

Lesson learned: if you like red roses and want fresh ones every day, don't give your husband a blow job.

Maybe this man has already gotten his daily sexual service out of the way, so all he has to do is buy the roses, or the chocolate, and go home to dinner with his wife and three children. That is, if they survived the latest pigua in Haifa.

The evening news will show the damage, gruesome pictures that get more so every day. The media's hunger for gore and blood is ever growing. The reporters push their cameras into someone's crying face, the way they do in

A Small Country about to Vanish

America. We are becoming desensitized, she thinks, chewing. We are slowly rotting from the inside out.

Something is about to break inside Rona. That image of the baby's head hasn't left her. Instead of numbing down, like everyone else, Rona has become a bundle of raw nerves. She feels everything too strongly, amplified beyond its function, like the volume of that last action film she watched.

When she sees people, they split open in her imagination. When talking to Gila and Mike, she pictures their body parts flying in the air. How long can she carry on like this?

She fixes her gaze on the man at the next table who has turned off his laptop, put his cellphone in his back pocket, and is getting up to leave. Suddenly agitated, she's compelled to yell out empty accusations at him for cheating on his wife.

"You . . ."

Rona realizes that she's pointing a finger at a total stranger and her face muscles are arranged in what feels like a twist of fury.

The man expresses kind concern. "Ha'kol be'seder?" he now asks Rona.

Her mind plays one of those tricks. She suddenly sees the man covered in blood, a large part of his skull missing. Then he becomes one piece again, a whole, healthy man with normal sexual urges.

Rona is filled with remorse. *We may all be dead soon.*

She says, "Go have your blow job," giving him permission.

Unfortunately, in Hebrew that verbal permission translates loosely into "Go fuck yourself," which is exactly the opposite of her meaning.

The man shakes his head. "*Me'shu'ga'at.*" Crazy. Rona hears him muttering to himself, "No wonder they blow us up. This country is full of insane people."

"That's what I say," Rona informs the cappuccino, hiding her face. She hopes the man isn't obliquely related to her, say, one of Mike's teachers who will recognize her at tonight's recital. Poor Mike doesn't need more reasons to be ashamed of his mother.

Daniella is very late. What's keeping her? Fear grips Rona in the middle of another bite, and for a second she stops the systematic grinding of food between her jaws. Was Dani in Haifa? She'll call her immediately after finishing the sandwich. It's best when still hot and when the cheese is mushy and stringy. Rona resumes her eating with a sense of religious mission.

The hunger grows inside her even as she imagines Daniella in ten million pieces.

Almost an hour late, Daniella shows up in one piece and wearing a two-piece Anne Klein suit she and Rona had chosen together a week ago.

"Sorry, motek," she says. "Cleaning up took longer than I thought."

Daniella has a live-in Filipina au pair, but there are certain cleaning chores she likes to do herself. Her Jung therapist diagnosed that particular behavior, and others, as obsessive compulsive disorder. Wonderful little Ana, whom Daniella loves as a sister, doesn't ever dust the bookcases or sweep behind the toilets. Ana has enough work taking care of Daniella and Asher's four sons.

"What if I don't come home at night," Daniella explains, "if I never come home, and Asher and the kids have to sit *shiv'a* and mourn me? The house will be full of people for seven days."

"If you die, no one would care about the toilets or the bookcases," Rona says, her mouth full. The sandwich itself is history, now the cucumber, the tomato and the olives all vanish into the cosmic-sized black hole inside her.

Daniella's bright red lipstick matches the strawberry brooch on her lapel. The jacket alone, blue with ivory pinstripes, cost twenty-four hundred shekels, the equivalent of six hundred dollars. The big purchases—houses, cars, Anne Klein items—are priced in American currency, as the shekel's value keeps dropping in brutal inflation. Rona could easily afford the whole suit, but couldn't wear it since it comes only in small and petite. When she was thin, such an ensemble was financially out of her reach. The irony makes her positively ravenous for another melted cheese sandwich. A pain begins in her stomach. She signals to the waitress to bring another order of the same thing.

"You look awful," Daniella says. "Those dark circles under your eyes. You should see Dr. Miller."

Daniella's plastic surgeon. Daniella is a social specimen, a perfect representation of Israeli upper middle class. An au pair, an acupuncturist, a plastic surgeon, a private yoga instructor, and a constant need to change Rona.

Those lips are huge, Rona thinks.

She closes her eyes and sees overlapping images: a baby's face drenched in blood and Eithan's dick covered in red lipstick. She tries to manipulate the pictures in her head into something less obscene. The baby's face should be covered with lipstick marks from all the kisses and love bestowed on her by her mother, aunts and her now dead grandmother. Eithan's dick should be blown to smithereens.

A second plate of food arrives.

"Eithan is having an affair," Rona says quickly, before she can change her mind and act as if life is perfect.

Daniella's hand, holding the cup of coffee, stops in midair.

Rona swallows a mouthful and says, "I saw lipstick on his *za'in*." She takes a large bite out of the cheesy part of the sandwich. She is still starving, and it isn't even time for her period.

"You sure it wasn't yours?"

"It was red and mine is purple. Besides, this wouldn't be my work. Not in last few years, anyway."

"Did you ask him?"

"I don't have to, Dani."

Daniella frowns at the plate in front of Rona. "You should lose some weight, see Dr. Miller and have those eye bags—"

Bang. Dishes rattle as Rona's fist meets the table. "You are not helping."

A spoon slides off to the floor, and Daniella bends over to pick it up.

In a sudden wish to hurt Daniella, Rona says, "They all do it. It's those Russian women."

"Asher doesn't," Daniella responds in self-defense.

"How do you know?"

"Whatever he wants, he gets from me."

"What does he want, Dani?"

"What they all want. Servicing a man is easier than servicing a car. They like to stare at tits and ass, but when all is said and done and the lights are out, all they want is a blow job. They want to lie back and do nothing."

As Daniella sips mud coffee, Rona locks her gaze on those pouty lips exaggerated by silicone injections into today's popular look. Women with totally normal lips pay to have them plumped-up by injections and end up looking deformed. This fashion of body modification reminds Rona of the Mursi women who stretch their lips with clay plates. The size of the plate is a measure of social importance. Daniella was just as appalled as Rona when they came across the photos of those mutilated women in National Geographic, yet what she does to her own face and body is just as grotesque. And that ridiculous, dark lip liner might as well be a drawn mustache. Daniella thinks it makes her sexier.

Red lipstick.

"Like a Mursi woman," Rona mutters.

"Like a what?"

"Nothing," Rona says. She should stop thinking out loud.

"Eithan is a handsome man," Daniella says, her gaze measuring Rona, making her feel naked and ugly. "Women want him."

The food rises into Rona's throat. "Do you?"

Daniella laughs. A lipstick mark adorns her white mug. It smears.

Rona stares at it and repeats, "Do you?"

"What, Eithan?"

"Yes, Eithan."

Daniella glances down at her mug and her enormous lips form a smile. She wipes the lipstick off the rim with a napkin. "Come on, motek. I'd clean up after myself."

"Right." Rona laughs and both of them relax.

She lets Daniella talk about her day, her children, the chemical peel she's planning for the fall, the sex she had with Asher the night before and how good it was. Daniella repeats, as if to convince herself, "Whatever he *could* get outside, he gets from me." She adds, "You and Eithan should see a sex therapist."

Lipstick on Eithan's dick. Birth control in Gila's backpack. Even Mike has a doe-eyed admirer. It seems everyone but Rona has sex.

Rona feels sick. The split inside her skull is getting wider and the headache starts. When she was a kid, those headaches got her out of the four-to-six piano practice. Eva had allowed her to lie down in the dark. Sometimes Rona would fake a migraine just to be left alone, but then she'd be stuck at home, unable to see her friends, and what's more, oppressed by Eva, who would hover with either hot tea or iced lemonade, depending on the season.

Daniella talks about a new art project—the materials she'll use, the technique, the style.

"I have a whole new show in mind," she says. "More content, less color and the subject is peace and war. You see? Peace first."

"Innovative," Rona says.

She enjoys Dani's art, but finds the process of making it boring. She doesn't want to know the how, so she lets her mind wander and takes a mental inventory of her life so far.

She has kept the same core of friends, as a substitute for the large family she'd never had as a child. Daniella has known her since kindergarten and they can read each other's minds. Asher can read Rona's mind, a fact that makes him argue with her before she opens her mouth. Eithan was her grade school sweetheart—no surprises there. Rona's brother lives nearby with his family. Her nieces and nephews, Eithan's brothers and their families, all pop in and out of her house without announcement. She loves them all, but there must be more out there. How can she get away from this claustrophobia, this totally predictable life?

She is fat and forty-nine, has dark circles around her eyes, but no wrinkles, maybe because of the fat. She cooks breakfast for the kids and Eithan every day. They go to school and work, and she eats the leftovers because she hates to throw away food.

Rona doesn't have to work for a living, so she cleans the house alongside Jihan, then plays the piano and eats the cookies from the jar on top of it. On weekends friends come over, couples she and Eithan have known since childhood or met during their military service. They all shout politics. Rona, the only lefty in the group, mostly disagrees with them, and their arguments drown hers. When they leave at around two in the morning, Eithan cleans up and goes to bed. Rona stays up and eats the leftovers.

She gave up a career, maybe fame, to take care of her kids and now that they're grown, they're embarrassed by the way she looks and dresses and eats anything that wouldn't eat her first.

The slim and fashionable Daniella is exactly Rona's age. She has help from Dr. Miller. Rona's children look up to her. Her career as an artist is blossoming. Her huge canvases are priced in dollars, thousands of dollars. Asher adores her and the lipstick on his dick is Daniella's shade of red.

Even Gila has betrayed Rona, discussing sex with Daniella and not her. Did Daniella play mom and suggest the birth control pills to her daughter?

"You haven't listened to a word I said." Daniella breaks into Rona's musings.

No, she hadn't.

This mall scene is getting on her nerves with its superficiality. All the people packing this place—shopping, dining, carrying on laughing conversations about mundane subjects such as plastic surgery, sex and fashion—they are all getting on her nerves.

A pretty Filipina woman passes their table, slim and quick with shiny black hair and smooth skin, a yellow plastic bag with the Candyland logo in her hand. Probably an au pair with temporary permit, working in Israel, sending money to feed her family back home.

Had she left her newborn baby with her aging parents? Rona can't bear to think of that little kid growing up motherless.

All that effort for food?

Rona's full, stretched stomach is about to burst. She wants to stop the woman and say, *Go back to the Philippines before this country of abundance devours you too. We're stuck here. You aren't.*

"Rona, motek, what's the matter?" Daniella cries out.

Slowly, Rona looks up at her. "A sex therapist for Eithan and me, a plastic surgeon for me, a gynecologist for Gila. What about Mike? What doctor should he see?"

"Rona, I don't understand—"

"What is this need you have to fix me and my family?"

"Calm down."

"Oh, I'm calm," Rona says. "Did Gila come to you for advice?"

"Yes," Daniella says. "I suggested that she see Dr. Rosenblatt and she did."

"Shouldn't her mother have a say?" Rona asks. "How dare you go behind my back."

"I thought I was helping. Gila was so distraught."

Rubbing it in like sandpaper on third-degree burns, Rona thinks. She can't actually say it, because the food threatens to erupt from her stomach. She envisions a giant cloud of disgusting particles showered on this pseudo-merry world of afternoon shopping.

Daniella rushes around the table and to her side.

"Sliha," Rona manages to say, meaning both *get out of my way* and *forgive me*.

She covers her mouth, grabs her purse and starts running.

A Small Country about to Vanish

15

Rona runs across the floor—passing tables, passing rows of discounted merchandise hanging on hooks outside stores, passing children on Rollerblades—to the closest place with a bathroom—Acapulco, the Mexican restaurant. She rushes through the busy dining area where it seems a big chunk of Tel Aviv is having an early dinner.

She gets to the ladies room, the vomit already filling up her mouth. She sees feet underneath the door of the first stall to the right, so she takes the second stall and, just in time, bends over the toilet, throwing up everything she's eaten since 1971.

Half collapsing, she holds her face in her hands, wishing she were dead. Her stomach hurts so much. She heaves and gasps, more and more coming out of her. She hears a man's sigh, an old sound from her own youth, and she keeps throwing up.

What's a man doing in the ladies room?

In her mind she sees the baby's head, half of it blown off in the ice cream parlor. She takes a deep breath to keep from blacking out. She slides to the floor, her head over the white bowl.

Another sigh, this time a woman's. Then "*da*" and more sighs and groans.

Rona opens her purse and searches for a wet wipe. As she cleans her face, she glimpses the blue edge of her passport, which she always keeps with her, a strange habit she picked up from Eva, who says things like, *A Jew should always be ready to relocate* and *You never know when you'll have to leave at a moment's notice with only the clothes on your back and your ancient Erard.*

Shoah Syndrome, Gila calls it.

The man groans again. Rona wonders when Eithan last made love to her with such passion. *When did I ever respond like this*? The woman makes throaty, unintelligible, rhythmic sounds of either pleasure or pain. This is not a fake orgasm.

Rona gets curious. Slowly she lowers her aching head until it nearly touches the dirty concrete floor, and peeks through the gap. A pair of Adidas, partially covered with crumpled blue jeans, a woman's manicured hand on the floor and a pair of red high heels. Daniella would know the make of the shoes. Rona doesn't, but she knows her color chart.

The shoes are the same shade of red as that fateful drag of lipstick.

Her vomit in the toilet stinks up the air, ruining what may be a couple's last sexual pleasure. And this is no quickie. It goes on and on. In her thoughtfulness, Rona flushes. A fatalistic tone has invaded all her actions. Whatever she does lately, she feels she's doing for the last time.

If I were a Palestinian boy or girl the age of either one of my children, she thinks, and I had no place to call home, nothing but an explosive belt around my waist, and an oppressive military force with uniforms and artillery came to my hometown and on a regular basis arrested and detained my brothers, my cousins and my father . . . If I were looking into this bourgeoisie scene, I'd see them eating tamales, drinking Margaritas and fucking in the toilets. They have beautiful homes and I have nowhere to go. So *kaboom*. No one is going home tonight. And body parts would fly around killing the Nazis along with me.

Wait. There are no Nazis and this time I'm the oppressive force, not the oppressed, at least according to the UN. So why do I feel that I have nowhere to go?

Sitting on the floor next to the toilet, listening to the noisy couple going on and on endlessly, Rona realizes she doesn't have a home. She takes another alcohol-saturated wipe out of her purse and runs it on her damp face, then down her throat a few times in a circular motion. An image of Eva scrubbing floors flickers through her mind.

That plush place in Savyon has never belonged to her. Eithan isn't hers, Mike and Gila are on an extended loan, soon to reach its maturity.

The couple finish and start again. Rona remains quiet, listening in longing, letting them enjoy, until a velvety voice says in Russian, "Do Svidaniya."

That could have been the end of it. Rona in her fairness would have let both of them leave in comfort, without intruding, but the man answers.

"The Korean place tomorrow."

His voice!

High heels click away. Rona stops wiping her face. She struggles to her feet, steps out, and stands face to face with the love of her life.

16

Marina's footsteps die down. Eithan zips up his pants. This was so much better than yesterday; tonight he'll buy Rona chocolate instead of roses. Milk chocolate, no nuts, the kind she likes the most. He takes a deep breath, shakes his testicles into place and steps out of the stall. His heart skips a beat.

Rona is very pale. She looks sick. Her puffy face is contorted with pain. *How is she here? How is Rona here?*

"She didn't even wash her hands," Rona says, surprising him with the composure of her voice.

"Oh," he says in the same hoarse voice that had just said, "Ahh."

"Nice to be multilingual," Rona says. "Do svidaniya, *Le'hitra'ot*, see you."

"Rona, I love only you," Eithan says.

"*Kus emak*," she blurts out the oft-used Arabic equivalent of *fuck you*. Poor Hebrew has to borrow insults from foreign traditions, one of the reasons the natives are so familiar with other languages.

Rona turns to leave, and Eithan follows, calling her name, wanting to pacify her. Yet he can't see her in the darkness of the packed Acapulco.

So much for buying her chocolate. He'll make it up to her, seriously apologize tonight after Mike's recital. There's no time to apologize now because they'll have to be ready soon and this is Mike's biggest night. Maybe she'll be more willing to forgive him after the recital, as the proud mom of a piano virtuoso.

A Small Country about to Vanish

He searches for a sight of her in the main concourse, even checks a few stores, but Rona is gone.

He leaves Avivim through the back entrance and hurries to his SUV. Everyone drives these monsters, despite the difficulty in finding parking spaces. There's no room to breathe in this smothering country, and gas prices are sky high. An SUV is a status symbol, and Eithan has earned his.

Eithan starts the car and, about to back out of his parking space, he hears the blast.

*

On the way to her car Rona feels a split, like the baby's head, half-dark, half-light with blood spreading in a widening circle from the inside out. The split, quiet and calm, opens wider just for her, like a door she never knew existed. As she crosses the threshold, lighter-than-air and strangely energized, all becomes clear. She had sprouted wings and she knows where to go next, and what to do. It's all up from here.

*

An explosion rocks the SUV and the mall behind Eithan. Not here. He is used to violence in the daily news, but not here in his neighborhood, not where his family hangs out every day. He pulls out his cellphone and, in a reflex manner, punches Rona's number first. Guilt-ridden, he hangs up. He'll call Gila first.

Gila's *hello* sounds sleepy.

"Are you okay? Where are you?"

"In bed, Aba. I don't feel well."

"Where's your brother?"

"Getting dressed for his show. What the matter?"

"I'll be home soon, motek. Turn on the news, another pigua."

He calls Tally.

She and her family are all fine. "Baruch Hashem," she adds the compulsory blessing.

He hesitates, then dials Rona's cellphone again. It rings, rings, rings, then her voice comes on, "I'm not available, leave a message."

Rona.

Not you.

He leaps out of the SUV and runs back, passing rows of parked cars, toward the mall. He's stopped by armed police.

The parking lot is in chaos, loud with screams and the sirens of emergency vehicles. All those years with Rona and now all is gone, turned into a puzzle that would never be put together. Those last angry words, were they the last he would ever hear from his wife? Regret, pain, horror. Normally he would have also called both his brothers, but Rona is the only one who matters now.

"My wife is inside," he says, trying to push his way through the security guards.

"You can't go in, sir."

Eithan understands that a second explosion may follow, another bomb, meant to kill the rescuers.

His phone rings. Rona. He picks up. His mother asks, "Ha'kol be'seder?"

"No." Hearing his mother's voice, Eithan becomes a boy again. He holds back the tears. And then he doesn't.

"It's Rona."

*

A Small Country about to Vanish

Gila turns on the news. Another one happened in the parking lot near a shopping mall. They don't say where.

It was one of the hottest days of the year and a man wearing a big coat attracted immediate attention. One of the shoppers, army sergeant Haddas Golan, on her way to buy a birthday present for her seven-year-old daughter, approached the man as he was about to force his way into the main entrance. She pulled a stylish, little silver gun out of her green Gucci purse and said, "Hands up," like in an old Western movie. He smiled at her with triumph and praised his God in Arabic, the familiar *Al'la hu akbar*. Seeing his hand reaching into the coat, Haddas Golan shot him once in the head just as he pulled a string and blew himself up. Ten were killed, among them Sergeant Golan herself, and more than a hundred were wounded. Many are still unaccounted for.

"It was a great miracle," Yoel Raviv says on television. "In her death, Sergeant Haddas Golan saved many lives. If it weren't for her quick actions, the man would have forced his way into the crowded mall and hundreds would have been killed."

"What a fucked-up country," Gila says to herself, measuring Nescafe into a blue Bugs Bunny mug. "Haddas Golan's seven-year-old daughter doesn't consider it a miracle."

She pours boiling water into the mug and stirs. She hasn't yet touched her homework for tomorrow, Mike's recital is in two hours, and she feels terribly tired. Sophie said the stuff she gave her would keep her up all night. Sophie's brother, a medical student in Jerusalem, had gotten it for them, but instead of helping her stay up, it made Gila sleepier.

"This time it happened in Avivim," says Yoel Raviv on the news, completing his report.

"Avivim? *Fuck*," Gila cries out.

Immediately awake, she picks up her cellphone and starts calling all her friends.

17

Eighty-year-old Eva sits at her old piano, caressing the keys as she would the face of a dying child. She glances around her daughter's grand living room, tears fogging up her big glasses. Such a beautiful house, she thinks, so well decorated, so elegant, and so unhappy, which is the real reason she refuses to move into the nice room they have ready for her. Eva, now widowed, is just fine living in her little apartment on the fourth floor.

The house has filled up with neighbors, family and friends. They've all heard, and now they're waiting for Rona to come home.

Uri pulls out a chair and sits next to Eva.

"It'll be all right, Mama," he says softly in Hungarian. "You'll see, Rona will walk in any minute."

All those years and still she doesn't speak much Hebrew. She could never pronounce the hard sounds like the sabres or find the right word. Eva asks Uri to turn off the TV. She can't stand the tears of pain and the images of devastation.

She touches the ivory keys with contorted, arthritic fingers —black, white, black, black, white, white—thinking of how she'd arrived at the port of Haifa in her twenties, burning with the spirit of a pioneer. She had the clothes on her back, her friend Ruth, and this very piano. It would have been easier to carry a flute or a violin, but she couldn't play those.

Black key, white key.

Losing Ruth had been the hardest, sharper and more unbearable for Eva than all the other losses, because she couldn't tell anyone what they'd meant to each other. When Ruthie was taken from her, shot by an Arab sniper in the Galilee, Eva had lost her center. She'd kept Ruth's sepia portrait on top of the piano for many years. Now the piano was here and she couldn't remember where Ruth's portrait was.

Eva's memories skip to that day she'd searched under Rona's mattress for banned music and found a diary. She shouldn't have read those Hebrew scribbles. Rona's handwriting reminded her of musical notes; she could almost sing a song to it. Eva had read one page, only to find out where Rona's hostility came from.

All she cares about is that stupid piano, Rona had written. *Not me or Uri or Aba or even her dead relatives. She abandoned them in Europe, didn't she? She should've brought them to Israel with her so I'd have living grandparents, aunts, uncles and cousins. Instead I have to play this monster.*

Eva couldn't identify every letter, every word, but that one paragraph pierced her heart like a dagger. Rona had no sympathy. Eva had told her the stories, but it was apparent that her daughter had never listened. Otherwise she would have seen the truth.

Eva had begged her parents to take her younger sisters and brother and come with her to the real homeland, but they were too complacent to give up the comforts of their civilized Europe.

"Palestine is a barren desert of scorpions and snakes," Eva's mother had warned. "You'll die of malaria and starvation."

"Israel, not Palestine," the young Eva had dreamily corrected.

Eva and her group of friends established a small settlement in the Galilee. They drained the swamps by planting eucalyptus trees. Eva was strong and lucky enough not to catch

A Small Country about to Vanish

malaria. She'd sometimes starved and she'd lost some friends —and her Ruthie—but she lived. Her parents, brother and sisters died of starvation in their civilized Europe, where the scorpions hid within uniforms and the snakes twisted into swastikas.

Now Rona may be lost to the same hatred.

Rona never had the drive, not the drive that had pushed Eva. Eva had to pressure her, threaten, even yell, to make her sit down and practice. Rona used to fake those headaches and she, Eva, had to fake all that extra care. Rona hated the attention. Eva did it—the tea, the lemonade, the hovering—to teach her lessons other than piano.

Uri has left her side and now her grandson Mike sits down and kisses her cheek. Mike is the real virtuoso of the family, but what's the meaning of those earrings and the tattoos? The new generation . . .

In broken Hebrew, she says, "Please, Mikey, play that piece I like on *this* piano."

"It needs tuning," he says.

"I know," Eva answers.

He remains next to Eva at the old Erard. His priorities have changed. The venue of his recital and the program have changed too. Instead of the planned Scriabin, he starts playing Eva's favorite, "The Moonlight Sonata."

Eva remembers sore knees, scrubbed floors and a stubborn girl with long black braids and a strange affinity for Wagner. She lets her tears flow freely with the graceful adagio sostenuto.

*

The packed living room—fifty or more—falls into a hush. This is Mike's big night. Most of his intended audience have gathered in this room. His family, his teachers, his friends and their families, and even more are flowing in through the open door.

Mike's thoughts are on his mother. *Ima, come home. I don't mind if you tell me off about my technique.* "The composer is God, don't make pauses where they're not intended" or "Your left hand is lazy and we have to do something about the thumb crossing." *Come and say something. I don't care if you nag me, Ima. I'm just a little boy and I need you so much. Please don't be in pieces.*

Today there's nothing wrong with Mike's technique. For the first time in his life he understands his mother's instructions to *play from your heart, not from your fingertips.*

*

Daniella prepares dinner and Uri helps. No one really wants to eat, but she needs to keep busy. She's still trembling, unable to talk about having just escaped Avivim with her life. She had remained at that small table sipping her coffee instead of following an angry, distressed and sick Rona. Would she have died with her had she been a better friend?

Daniella's husband has reported to the emergency room in Tel-Hashomer to tend the victims. No one called him back for duty—he's the head of the department—but that's what you do if you're a doctor, a nurse, a janitor, when you hear about a pigua in your district.

Not a word from Rona. Daniella had watched her gorging herself at Café International. Would that be the last image she'd hold of her childhood friend? And that ugly argument between them, Rona accusing Daniella of stealing Gila's affection.

A Small Country about to Vanish

The truth: Daniella, who has four sons, wishes she had a daughter like Gila. It's also true that Gila asked her for advice, seeing the cool Daniella as a replacement for the more conservative Rona. But Gila isn't a baby who can be stolen. Look at her, seated between two adoring friends, all grown up.

Daniella wipes off a tear, her longing gaze fixed on Gila. If indeed Rona is gone, she may have no choice but to act as this girl's mother. A glimmer of pleasure surfaces. A speck. The speck is as tiny and vulnerable within this immense loss as the State of Israel is within the vast Middle East.

Sorrow overcomes her, and Daniella starts crying into the salad bowl, her tears adding salt to the balsamic vinegar.

Through a mist she sees Eithan, frantically dialing his cellphone. Call after call, his face more ashen with each hang up. Daniella can't help imagining the smear of red lipstick that had upset Rona. Is it still there? Now his eyes are also red, his gaze on the door. He is stoic.

A big, muscular, athletic macho man doesn't cry.

Daniella says, "Watermelon? An orange? Some chicken?"

*

Eithan shakes his head no and keeps dialing the emergency rooms of every hospital in Tel Aviv. Beilinson. Ichilov. Tel Hashomer.

"Did you admit a Rona Rosenthal?" Eithan repeats the same question.

When Rona makes her entrance, he wants to be the first to see her reaction. After all, Mike is playing more beautifully than ever. Rona should hear that. She should see her beautiful son baring his heart through his fingers.

Eithan doesn't want the police to come, asking him to identify body parts.

He makes a pledge to himself: if Rona walks in the door, everything will change.

He hears his son's playing. He sees his daughter seated on the stairs between her two closest friends. Most people have one shadow, Gila has two—Ramón and Sophie—competing for her love and attention. The three of them are huddled on the stairs together, a three-headed entity, serious and giggly all at once, the way only teenagers can be. They remind Eithan of three other school kids from many years ago. Rona was the center, and Eithan and Shelli followed her like admiring shadows. Eithan had won the ultimate prize, and now he has lost it. Where's Shelli today?

*

Ramón on her left, Sophie on her right, Gila tries to be brave, because crying will be an affirmation of her mother's death.

Ima will come home soon, she has to. There's no life without her. Gila recalls the hurt in her mother's face when she waved the package of Estrostep at her. What if she'd confessed the truth right there and then, would Ima have understood her predicament? Now more desperate than ever, Gila wishes she had asked for advice. Dear Dani thought she was helping, yet Gila hadn't told her the truth.

Ramón's hand squeezes her shoulder, warm and reassuring. She sneaks a peek at his imperfect profile and melts with love for him. He's listening to the music, immersed in it, yet still gripping her shoulder as if to say, *Whatever sorrow awaits you, I'll take away some of it.*

Gila glances to the right, at Sophie, who senses the glance and returns it. Sophie with her tough façade and all those tattoos and rings—in her nose, tongue, one on the eyebrow, and a hidden one enclosed in folds of soft flesh. Sophie's eyes are tender, so tender, telling Gila, *I'll take care of you. If you're left alone in the world, I'll be your mother, father and sister.*

Mike's friends also surround him with a protective shield.

A slew of boys and girls are arranged at his feet by the piano. That little hottie has an obvious crush on him. Now Gila wants to laugh at how the girl tries to rearrange her breasts into a cleavage, believing no one can see what she keeps doing, all for her brother's benefit. The girl's small tzitzies keep disappearing into her blouse. The effort is wasted on Mike, who is too involved in his slow, pretentious music. Gila digs both her elbows into her best friends, who read her mind. The three of them snicker at how the girl gazes at Mike, eyes dreamy, her intentions blatant.

The slow part of the sonata is done, and Mike goes into the fast movement. Gila stops giggling. Mike and Rona call it the allegretto. Gila knows more than she cares to know about music, but she hates how Mike and her mother use technical terms in a way that makes her feel like an outsider. She listens with new interest, and she forgets to be annoyed with Mike's divine aura, that god-among-the-mortals imaginary cloak he's been wearing ever since his bar mitzvah, exactly a year ago. She didn't know he had this music in him, this talent. In one hour he has grown up.

Is Mike also torn by a problem only Ima can solve for him? The girl with the crush on him begins to cry.

Gila hides her face between her knees. She thinks of the nursery rhyme Rona used to sing for her many years ago.

I'm not a crybaby, but why, Ima, why are the tears crying by themselves?

18

Eithan stands at his kitchen's door, facing his garden and olive trees, facing away from those who are confirming Rona's absence with their presence, away from Uri and Daniella who are busy arranging sandwiches on a large silver tray. He strokes the old dog's head, Max, who is alert for once, aware of his master's distress.

The summer breeze carries in the fragrance of geranium and roses from the garden.

Rona, come enjoy these smells with me.

An African grey parrot stares at Eithan sideways from the olive tree. Yossi, the neighbor's bird, is allowed to fly out of his cage in the evenings and listen to Rona and Mike practice piano. Yossi can't sing *Tristan ünd Isolde* in German beginning to end, as the joke goes, but when the muse swoops in on him, he sings random Wagner arias. The ninety-five-year-old Frieda brought him with her from Frankfurt before the shoah. Over sixty years together, Frieda and her bird have bonded as one.

Sadly, Yossi will survive his Frieda, therefore Eithan—who has also survived his beloved—feels sudden sympathy with the bird. The bird's affinities are directed toward the piano, as the two are both musical intermediaries lugged from Europe to Israel in the 1920s.

Behind Eithan, in a living room packed with friends and family, Mike starts playing the allegretto. In reaction to the changing rhythm, Yossi breaks into gaudy singing of the "Liebestod." Rona would have laughed out loud at this irony.

Eithan only smiles. *Liebestod* means love-death. It's Isolde's swan song and Rona's favorite aria.

Through a film of tears, Eithan looks out to the night, to his own vast garden, and for a moment he has a feeling of total estrangement from the familiar surroundings. *Jamais vu*, the opposite of *deja vu*. The world without Rona is a different planet, unknown to him. She's not even confirmed dead, yet he grieves as if she were. His wife, his playmate, his first and last love, his advocate. Once, Rona had protected him. The system tried to expel him, but Rona intervened and he was given another chance.

Yossi the parrot sings Isolde's words. *Seht ihr's, Freunde? Seht ihr's nicht?* Can't you see my friends? Do you not see?

Rona was the first one who believed in him, spoke in his favor, asked their friends, *Can't you see how wonderful he is? Am I the only one*?

Although religion isn't a significant part of Eithan's life, he has the intrinsic urge to drop to the floor and tear his clothes in a traditional expression of grief for the dead. He settles for less drama and leaves his clothes intact when he collapses. He feels the chill of marble penetrating his slacks. Rona was right about marble making the hot, humid climate more tolerable. This natural stone with the gold vein was imported from Italy at her insistence. It seemed borderline pathological to him how she saved her pennies on small items, milk and bread, while squandering hundreds of thousands on floors, windows, art and furniture.

Don't think of Rona in the past tense. She isn't dead at all. No, his Isolde will come in any minute now and embrace him, forgive him.

Arms are wrapping around him, but not Rona's plump ones. Bony, thin arms. Daniella has joined him on the floor.

She clings to him, rocking him, crying with him. "Eithan, Eithan, Eithan," she says, and her voice is full of knowledge.

He knows Daniella knows because Isolde—no, Rona—told her. Daniella's voice is full of compassion. She has already forgiven him.

Yossi keeps singing the "Liebestod" from the olive tree, Eithan and Rona's swan song. No, *Tristan ünd Isolde*'s song.

Daniella rocks him in her arms, repeating, "Eithan, Eithan," as if her vocabulary stopped with his name.

Grief, like sex, robs our brains of words, he thinks.

For all he knows, Marina has died in this pigua, but somehow it's none of his business. Marina belongs to the part of his body he is about to tie into a knot and forget. Marina has Alexei, the big mafia man, to cry for her. Eithan had seen Alexei once, actually a tiny man, in a shiny, black, eighty-thousand-dollar Mercedes Benz. His bigness stemmed only from the potential of his actions.

"I don't know why I . . ." Eithan chokes up.

Daniella keeps rocking him, shushing him, whispering, "Eithan, Eithan" in his ear and crying. Or is she saying Tristan, Tristan?

Now he wants her to stop, because her crying only confirms what he refuses to accept.

"Listen." He steadies Daniella. "Can you hear?"

"The bird is singing Wagner," Daniella simply says and nothing is wrong with her vocabulary. Her brown eyes are familiar, intelligent, when she puts a hand under Eithan's chin. "I would have divorced Asher for less. You fucked up."

"Big time," Eithan agrees.

He plans to talk to Asher and suggest that he stop before it's too late. Stop cheating on Daniella with the gold-toothed Svetlana, he'll tell his friend.

Eithan and Asher have shared their two mistresses. Once, in a little orgy—Marina's idea. He thinks of all the combinations they tried that night at the Hilton. First it was Eithan and Marina, Asher and Svetlana, in separate beds, in the dark and under the covers. Then the covers came off, the lights came on, and Marina jumped in with Svetlana. The two started kissing, whispering in Russian, laughing softly, playing together as if they really enjoyed it. Of course the women did it only to turn on their exhausted men, who were ready to call it a night.

Then—Eithan winces at the memory, but it did happen—he and Asher formed an unplanned union, also with the covers off, in full light, forgetting about the women in the next bed. Although Eithan won't admit it even to himself, the memory of that night has since fed and intensified his orgasms.

Later, when they told and retold the story to their green-with-envy buddies, they left out that unintended combination. In their rehashing, Asher and Eithan remained the passive spectators of a live "blue show." Between themselves, Eithan and Asher blamed their homosexual encounter on the hard liquor, the hashish and the sight of those beautiful women with their faces shoved like a pair of vacuum cleaners in each other's pussies.

"Eat something." Daniella's voice lands him back in reality. "You have to be strong for the kids and for Eva."

"All right." Eithan also feels guilty on Daniella's behalf.

"Rona never knew," Daniella says, getting up.

"Knew what?"

"How she influenced my every decision. She was the force behind every success."

"Is," Eithan corrects. He's not giving up on Rona.

"You see, it's a nagging childhood neurosis. I look up to Rona, I try to impress her."

"She has that influence on people," Eithan says.

"The plastic surgeries," Daniella says, gesturing at her face, "the art, the clothes I wear. I wanted to have more children than Rona, a larger house, a wider garden. Stupid, isn't it? Rona used to be the queen."

"She still is," Eithan says.

Rona loomed over all of them in Eithan's mind. No one measured up. She had always been larger than all of them. But that she'd never known.

Uri's jaw is set in that rigid expression, ready to face any calamity. For a moment, just by the way his lips form those thin, white lines, he resembles his sister. He smiles at Eithan, also like Rona, and hands him a roast beef sandwich.

"Split it with me," Eithan says, standing up.

Uri cuts the sandwich somewhere in the middle, and hands Eithan the larger half. Both men stand, chewing, their backsides against the marble kitchen counter, also Rona's choice. Also imported.

Mike suddenly stops playing, the bird stops singing, and Gila rushes to Eithan and clings to him. "Aba, why the fuck are they here?" she whispers.

Eithan turns to look at the new arrivals and nearly chokes on a mouthful of sandwich.

Tally's husband, Moishe, darkly clad, is surrounded by a group of men—the *minyan*. They're already gathering by the large window in the living room, opening their prayer books, covering their heads with talits and swaying forward and back like a field of black and white tulips in the wind. They are a force of nature, acting as if they belong in this completely secular home.

Tally has joined them. She stands separated from the men by a few steps, holding an open book, praying for her mother.

A Small Country about to Vanish

"Aba, say something," Gila protests. "They can't just take over our house like this."

Eithan is ready to kick them out, when Moishe approaches him. "May Ima come back in peace, God willing," he quietly says, and his words make Eithan feel strange gratitude. "Do you mind if we pray?"

"Go ahead," Eithan says. "If it doesn't help, it won't hurt."

"Would you like to pray with us?"

"No, Moishe," Eithan says, now choking on tears. "But thank you."

"I will," Uri says.

He joins them in prayer for his sister's safe return home. As he doesn't have a yarmulke and hasn't worn one since his own bar mitzva thirty years ago, he covers his head with the palm of his hand.

The men's voices fill the room with meditative chanting.

"Aba, why are you allowing this?" Gila cries out.

"Think of it as music," Eithan says. "Your mother loves music."

"But, Aba . . ."

"Let them be," he says, embracing her.

Gila relaxes in his arms. People start walking in and out of the kitchen, eating, talking in subdued tones about Rona. Other men join the minyan, all praying for Rona.

Yes, Rona was, is, always the center.

Gila looks up at him. "Are you okay?"

"Sure, motek," he says, although he's far from being okay. "Your Ima will come home, I'm sure."

Gila returns to her friends. Sophie opens her arms and clings to her as if she, Sophie, is the one in need of comforting. A new realization hits Eithan. Poor Sophie is in love with Gila. He thinks of the early seventies and that Shelli who had adored Rona, loved her desperately, hopelessly—and had lost.

He still remembers, and when he forgets, Asher and Gidi remind him of that fateful day they had all walked in on the girls in Rona's small room. Instead of the "Liebestod," it had been Demis Roussos singing the schmaltzy "Ever and Ever." Rona and Shelli had both been naked. In the light of that macramé-covered lamp, Eithan had seen arms and legs in intricate positions, fingers and lips in places he never knew were supposed to be included in lovemaking. He certainly learned a few ideas from that split second of action.

He recalls the girls' closeness, the bewildered expressions on their faces, the strange thrill he had felt and his embarrassment, as if the scene had somehow reflected on him. Asher and Gidi, who followed closely behind him, later teased him to death by singing that loathsome Roussos song.

Rona had pushed Shelli away and immediately said to Eithan, "I was just practicing, so I can do it with you."

"You weren't just practicing," said the hurt Shelli. "You liked it when I did the same to you."

Shelli had quickly covered herself with Rona's favorite pink dress—also Eithan's favorite for the easy access it provided to Rona's bra clasp. He hasn't seen the dress since that moment Shelli pulled her long dark hair back into a ponytail and raced from the room, slamming the door behind her.

Afterward, Rona tried to pacify him, believing he'd been angry. He'd let her have her belief, but in his fantasies, the girls always played for him, wore each other's dresses for him, practiced piano fingering on each other *to please him*.

Eithan wishes he knew what happened to her, to Shelli. Would she have felt the same pain at losing Rona-the-center?

Part Three
TRANSFIGURATION

A Small Country about to Vanish

19

To her family, Rona died. To herself, she lives. At least she isn't dead in the ordinary sense. She's undergoing verklärung, transfiguration, like Isolde of the "Liebestod."

When Rona left her cheating husband in the toilet of Acapulco, her stomach was empty and she was light on her feet. Riding down the escalator, she saw the familiar bird's-eye view of Tel Aviv in the early evening light. On a normal day this would have been the time to start piano practice, but today wasn't a normal day because of something that used to be the center of her being and wasn't anymore.

Why wasn't it a normal day? She vaguely remembered and it didn't matter.

The bird slowly swooped all the way down to the parking lot of Avivim. This city was hers, its night and day, its ancient buildings, its contemporary high-rises, its old and young people, its mixture of languages, its impossible traffic and the loud music blaring from the cars. This time Rona had no doubt. Tel Aviv was hers and she was saying goodbye to it.

Rona intended to turn right, toward her parked Fiat, but the split inside her head was growing fast, spreading wider—light as day on the left, dark as night on the right. A door opened wide before her, and when she entered, she knew the right choice. She chose daylight and turned left toward the taxicabs lined up on the corner. She got into the first one, sat next to the driver, and said, "Ben Gurion, please."

The driver, a dark-skinned man with a day-old beard, asked, "No luggage?"

"No," she said with urgency. "Just go. Please."

20

The cab, an old Mercedes model from the early eighties, rattles and clanks as it makes the turn into the autostrada, the fast four-lane road leading to the airport.

Nothing matters. Within moments a new daze has taken Rona's mind and soul and she is soaring in this newness. Avivim, Eithan and his Russian woman are far behind, now part of her past.

An Arabic station is playing a female singer trilling and longing for her beloved homeland. "*Baladi, ya baladi . . .*"

A brass plaque above Rona's head announces the driver's name in Hebrew, Arabic and English. Gibril abu Amal. There's so much information on that plaque and such pride. His name is Gibril, but everyone calls him Abu Amal after his firstborn. The man probably has many sons and daughters, and respect from all of them.

"My homeland, oh, my homeland . . ." The singer continues her ballad.

Gibril and his ancestors have lived in this land for many generations. Rona is only first-generation Israeli, her kids are second. Gibril travels much less out of his country, if at all, although hypothetically he can travel in all directions. He can cross north to Lebanon, east to Jordan or Syria, south to Egypt and west. Rona, who escapes the country any chance she gets, can only travel in one direction, west toward the Mediterranean. Gibril speaks her language very well, while she only understands snippets of his, including some choice expressions she wouldn't dare use in his presence.

A Small Country about to Vanish

Which one of them, Rona or Gibril, has more freedom of movement in this country, more love for it or deeper roots?

These existential questions keep bothering Rona out of pure habit. She looks out the window and back at her city, now in the distance and getting smaller. Goodbye, she says to it. Goodbye. Baladi ya Baladi.

"You want the news?" the driver asks, his fingers on the dial, ready to change the station for her.

"I'm sick of the news, Gibril," Rona says. "Let Om-Kalthoom sing."

"You know Om-Kalthoom?" Gibril is pleasantly surprised. "You people don't like Arabic music."

"I like all music," Rona says truthfully.

It's music night, she now remembers, Mike's recital. She's missing her son's big event. She so looked forward to it and now it comes as an afterthought and it will happen without her. She won't be there to smile and congratulate Mike and worry for him. She opens her mouth to ask Gibril to turn around and take her home, to her son, to her family.

Tel Aviv disappears in the distance and with it, her wish to turn back.

The highway stretches over open fields in unpopulated land that looked the same two thousand years ago. So much bloodshed later, and nothing has changed. Each lost life is like pissing in the ocean.

Without actually listening to the news, the conflict is in the air, in the voice of Om-Kalthoom singing "ya baladi," in the aroma of the cigarette smoke engulfing Rona, ingrained in every fiber of the seat beneath her. She hopes Gibril won't start talking politics. Normally she wouldn't mind—her opinions are probably not far from his—but not now.

Arab cab drivers and their Jewish customers have a way of politely discussing the news. It has to do with relieving the mind of any suspicion. An olive branch is offered by both sides and they always agree with each other, at least on the surface and while on the road. For the man at the wheel, it's an acceptable roundabout method of soothing the client's mind. As if saying, *I'm not a freedom fighter who would kidnap you and murder you and deliver your dismembered corpse to your loving family. I'm just a cab driver, making a buck.*

Vast fields extend on both sides of an empty highway.

Why is the highway to the airport empty this time of day? This emptiness on a road that is always jam-packed with traffic has the feel of a parallel reality, a passageway between two worlds. Rona's heart is throbbing in sudden fear. Is she dead? Is this person, this driver, not really a driver, not really whom that fake plaque announces him to be, Gibril abu Amal, but rather archangel Gabriel deceiving her into believing that she is on the way to the airport while all the while leading her to . . .

Where is she going?

She puts her hand on her chest. Of course she is alive, a fact verified by her heart's hurried pounding. She calms down again. This is not a Hollywood movie.

In the distance she sees grounded military aircraft. A Star of David is drawn in charcoal on a brick wall of a warehouse-like structure, and underneath a proud message reminds "Am Israel Hai." Even the walls here scream, "We are alive, don't forget it."

Her last doubts dissipate. As a fugitive Rona feels more alive than ever.

The walls always talk to us, only here The Star of David has replaced the swastika.

Gibril says, "Times have changed. It's hard to make a living these days."

"Yes," Rona agrees absentmindedly.

A Small Country about to Vanish

"I have a wife and five children in Daliat El Carmel. I just want to feed them."

Daliat El Carmel, a village in the Carmel range. In his own code, the man is telling her, *I'm not the sort of an Arab you should fear. I'm a Druse.*

She should participate in the conversation, so as not to offend him. This man has suffered discrimination all his life, from both Arabs and Jews. He looks like an Arab, talks like one and lives more like an Arab than a Jew. The Jews mistake him for an Arab, the Muslims call him a Jew because he and his grown children serve in Tzahal, the Israeli Defense Force. He is treated with skepticism by all.

"We, the little people," says the Druse, "want only to support our families. The politicians are the real problem, and we are eating their bullets. All those big men have bodyguards. We don't, so we blow up in the streets for them."

"Right," Rona says.

The Druse is turning the conflict into *us* against *them*. Small, inconsequential, espresso-sipping, ice-cream-licking, cab-driving individuals against the leaders with their limos and their bodyguards. Rona, while letting him talk, knows the simple truth. It's Arabs against Jews. It was Nazis against Jews. It was the Romans against the Jews. The ancient Greeks . . .

The Jews irk everyone. And with Eithan and his lipstick-smeared dick on her mind, Rona is ready to join the United Nations and hate the whole circumcised lot of them.

Not that she hates Eithan, or Israel with its difficult people. She will always love him, forever love this impossible country. She has become who she is because of Eithan and because of this country, but enough is enough. Her path is clear. She'll decide on a destination, buy a one-way ticket with one of her many credit cards and stock up on supplies at the duty-free shops upstairs.

They pass one of the airport's parking lots, the first sign of population. Gibril the Druse keeps talking. Rona doesn't want to hear anything about the Conflict.

Rona is getting away not only from her husband, her friends, her ungrateful kids, but also from the news and from that grueling, punishing, constant tension in the air. She wants a calm place, somewhere in the world where there are no Jews or Arabs and therefore no politics. Is there such a place? Someplace safe from any scrap of news. From even a newspaper.

Her passport could take her to Canada, New Zealand, Australia, USA. From her point of view, all those wonderful places are as relaxing as an American TV sitcom.

Rona used to be addicted to *The Brady Bunch*, to its mundane problems and its unvarying moods. Those kids were perfect because they never had to listen to Holocaust stories or hear supersonic booms blast over their heads. Mr. Brady didn't have to physically protect his six kids by fighting endless wars, and of course there was Florence. Or Carol. The Brady mom, bright and smiling, never yelled at Marcia and that cute little Cindy. Rona used to lie in bed at night and fantasize about Florence Henderson being her real mother, about her coming to tuck Rona in. She imagined herself living in that big house with all the stairs and the bickering kids instead of in the tiny apartment on the fourth floor with its old piano and her mother's ghosts.

It's five o'clock when Gibril arrives at Ben Gurion airport and stops at the gate for the first security check. The armed guard eyes him with initial hesitation, nothing obvious, just a brief lock of the gaze. He sees Rona, smiles and waves them through.

A Small Country about to Vanish

Life could have been different, Rona realizes, if only the Jewish people had agreed to establish a new homeland on another piece of real estate. They could have found another unwanted desert and made it blossom, could have built a New Jerusalem anywhere. But, no, they had to shed tears for the land of their origin. They had to return to their own history of hostility and persecution because her people flourish under pressure. A new land, untainted by wars and ghosts, may have opened up a new page for them, independent of Europe and the Middle East. She could have grown up strolling the beaches of New Zealand, learning to swim in the Pacific. What a dream.

Or, more likely, the Maoris would have learned to hate us like the rest of the world.

Gibril stops his cab at the terminal. "Have a safe trip," he says.

Rona pays him, including an unusually large tip, figuring that he deserves every shekel and more for simply showing up to work every day, never knowing what he'll face from his fares.

The old Rona would have chosen to drive her own car to the airport to save just a few shekels, but Rona's decision to leave her Fiat behind is the first step in her transformation. She intends to be different, to make different choices.

She's a new Rona who will choose convenience over money, light over darkness, and life over death.

21

Tired night passengers drag suitcases onto carts and approach the terminal. They all have luggage, tickets and destinations. Rona has none of the above. She sees her reflection in a wall of mirrors, still wearing the black Armani, now sporting a dry stain of vomit on her right shoulder.

No wonder Eithan gets it on the side, she thinks, playing devil's advocate. She normally has no use for devil's advocates, since the devil does a fine job advocating for himself.

Here's Steimatsky, a branch of the nationwide bookstore. She goes in. She finds a world atlas by a display of travel literature—books of photographs about Jerusalem, the Galilee, archeology in the Middle East.

She lifts the heavy atlas off the shelf and drops it; the thud causes heads to turn. A woman with platinum curls glances up. She's about Rona's age, much slimmer, wheeling a huge lime-green suitcase behind her while balancing a pile of books under one arm, as if unable to make up her mind what not to purchase.

A real book lover, Rona thinks. A kid in a candy store.

Rona opens the atlas at the polar projection, the North Pole, to outwit herself. Just before she flips a shekel, she searches for Israel. If one doesn't know where to look, one can't find it. Israel is located at the adjoining point of three continents, holding them together like a three-pronged hook. Or maybe Israel is forcing them apart.

Her country is too small for more than the first two letters, and even those are written outside its borders, on the blue background of the Mediterranean Sea. Israel is physically too small for representation on the world's map and politically too large, too volatile to maintain its own existence.

A small country, like Rona, about to vanish. And who would care?

Where can she go?

Coin in hand, she thinks of her wish list, which is more a list of prohibitions than one of choices: diplomatic relations with Israel (essential for the purpose of entry), no Jews or Arabs in overwhelming numbers, running hot water. She flips the shekel. It falls on the Nubian Desert, which fits none of the categories on her list. She flips again and gets a spot by Vienna. Can't get any closer to Beethoven's spirit, but other spirits, living and dead, are there. The *Anschluss*, the Wehrmacht, the *achtung*s and the 1940s in general make her groan. She flips again, and the coin falls on Acapulco de Juarez. How appropriate. She smiles, tapping that spot on the map. She'd escaped the Acapulco restaurant and Acapulco de Juarez will embrace her. There's a rhythm of a song here somewhere.

Now, reading material. She places the atlas back on the shelf and picks up a nice-looking little book about the ghosts of Berlin. Here's another one, from the same publisher, about the ghosts of Bergen-Belsen. She sees the word *Buchenwald* on one of the titles and doesn't touch the book.

What mortal wounds must have inspired those novels! Sixty years after the shoah and they're still writing about it, explaining the inexplicable. Why try? Wouldn't comprehending the act of murder make you one with the murderer?

She examines book after book of fine original Hebrew literature by well-known authors: Savyon Liebrecht, Meir Shalev, Amos Oz, Etgar Keret. Even the new novels or short story collections are Holocaust related, books by young authors who didn't experience it in person, but who, like Rona, were force fed the tales of the previous generation.

A flight to Warsaw is announced in Polish, then in Hebrew. The two languages warp in Rona's mind into a hybrid, a deformity. Here's a paperback, written by a high school girl who visited the camps on a class field trip. Rona opens it gingerly, expecting to be disgusted, as she would when tasting a piece of loathed food.

She reads an excerpt.

The perfumed tissue pressed against my face didn't block the smell of disinfectants. The ceiling was so low, Tommy and Ron had to bow their heads. In the corner, I saw a rusted container, slightly larger than those cans of pickles my mother opens for dinner. I'm told the can used to contain Zyklon B. Above me, where the gas had hit, the ceiling was stained blue. I'll never wear blue again. I'll never eat anything that comes out of aluminum cans. All around me I saw lines on the walls. They told us those were fingernail scratches. I looked down at my own pink-painted fingernails. I'll never complain. I'll never sleep.

Rona shuts the book in horror and reads the blurb on the back cover. *A fresh view of the shoah by a brilliant and insightful young author*.

As if the world needed another fresh view of what should have been buried long ago.

The school field trips to Poland and Germany were Rona's greatest pet peeves. Those so-called educational trips were the equivalent of teaching Marcia Brady how to use an Uzi submachine gun when all she needed was a pedicure.

Why not take those kids to art museums and chocolate factories? Everyone knows the history. Haven't they heard— hadn't Rona heard—millions of stories through plugged ears? Haven't they seen those old black and white documentaries?

Rona thinks of the skeletal bodies—some dead, some still moving—shoveled like garbage into mass graves. Those lives had become only as important as their after-product—perfectly organized ghastly mountains of eyeglasses, hair, gold teeth.

Young people should occupy their minds with beauty, sex and romance, not with the ugly past of victimhood.

Ever since the borders of Eastern Europe opened to Israeli citizens, they've been drawn back in droves. Organized groups visit the camps. Soldiers in uniforms, schoolchildren, *families*. They march from Auschwitz to Birkenau singing protest songs and carrying Israeli flags, a sort of "We're here and fuck you" to the descendants of the murderers.

They call it The March of the Living, but to Rona it seems like a freakish ritual of death. Particularly the way they all cram into those claustrophobic gas chambers and say the Kaddish, turning the prayer for the dead into an affirmation of their young existence. She doesn't understand the elevation of one's pride simply at the state of being alive. They buy German cars, shoes, television sets because the goods are there for the buying. Shouldn't they also take life for granted?

When it was Gila's turn to visit Poland with her classmates, Rona had refused to give her permission. The mental picture of her children, so well-fed and brimming with chutzpah, having to bend their heads under the low ceiling of a gas chamber—even in a demonstration of strength and sixty years later—was loathsome in her eyes.

Her mother had fled, preserving the family line. Why should her kids return to the death camps and become poisoned? What would be the value of that?

Eithan argued in favor of the trip, tried to change her mind. "Gila's friends are going. Why make her different?"

Rona then recalled a long-ago classroom scene, their friends following orders, ganging up on Eithan. Rona alone had refused to add twigs to the fire of persecution.

"Because Gila *is* different and one day she'll be proud of it," Rona had said to Eithan. "Your lambs-to-slaughter mentality caused the Holocaust in the first place."

Rona remained stubborn and Gila didn't go to Poland. That had started Gila's hostility toward Rona.

Rona puts all the shoah novels back on the shelf. Then she sees the yellow paperback, *Salamandra*. A gasp escapes her throat. Then, "Oh . . ."

22

I roll my lime-green carry-on behind me and wonder what to do with three hours to kill in Ben Gurion. Should I have a sandwich? A drink at the bar? Books win. I raid Steimatsky and browse the rack of Hebrew books, gathering past favorites into a pack under my arm.

I hear a gasp. And then, "Oh . . ."

I look up and see the woman in black, the one who moments ago acted erratically, dropping or flipping coins over an atlas. She's pressing a yellow book to her chest. Her eyes are shut, her lips are as white as her knuckles. The hand clutching the book is slim, but the adjoining wrist is magnified. My gaze follows a fat arm in a black sleeve up to the crest of a proud shoulder, up to a double chin, up to the face—swollen, tired and pale, dotted with faded freckles.

Her gray hair is short and stylishly cut. She's overweight, but not unattractive. Her black dress and the jacket over it seem expensive, soft-textured, as is the blue purse slung from her shoulder. A huge diamond ring adorns the middle finger of that unusually slim hand.

Those hands with the long fingers, that mix of elegance and melancholy in her posture, remind me of someone, stir the trace of memory from my past. My heart starts racing. I stare, fascinated, knowing that I may be intruding on a private moment. I argue that it isn't really rude because the woman in black hasn't noticed me. She stands frozen, attentive, as if a sad story is pouring into her ear, and she has no choice but to listen.

She mouths a word I can't identify.

*

Salamandra was the only book about the Holocaust Rona had agreed to read as a teen. Her former friend had talked her into reading it. Shelli had been fascinated with the stories of Ka-Tsetnik.

Rona wants to fling *Salamandra* with disgust against the rest of them, but she holds it tightly against her chest. What did Shelli use to say? Rona searches her head, mentally grasping the end of a brittle string leading to a fragment of a memory she had suffocated to death long ago.

A woman's voice announces a flight to Lisbon in Portuguese. From the corner of her eye, Rona sees others browsing. She hears the whispering of flipping pages, pages containing life stories. Those who tell those stories are desperate to tell. Those who read, not so desperate to know. Those who read—or are forced to listen—are sometimes desperate for silence.

Shelli wanted, needed, to know. Rona hugs the small book tighter, thinking *Shelli*.

More memories surface. How Shelli's mother had banned Ka-Tsetnik's books the way other parents banned Playboy magazine. Since banning a thing only makes it even more attractive, Shelli became obsessed. Rona used to check those books out of the library for her friend, a few at a time, as Shelli was a voracious reader and would devour the same book again and again, right there in the street or in Rona's room. Shelli had so adored Rona, but that adoration had gone a step too far.

Still, Rona could use some adoration at this point in her life, even the kind that goes too far. She hugs the book, now mouthing *Shelli*.

A Small Country about to Vanish

Shelli had been different from the slew of Rona's brazen friends, and Shelli was sacrificed, cut from her life, simply because she'd loved Rona too much. It was awful at the time, the only time Rona had joined the mob. Yet what choice had she had but to conform and hide in Eithan's arms and in that cloud of cool friends?

Now, the book tight to her chest, Rona regrets not having defended Shelli the way she had Eithan.

My conforming is over, Rona decides. I'm forsaking all my responsibilities, my cool friends, my ungrateful family, ready to reclaim our friendship, ready to accept your love and love myself again. Where are you, Shelli? It would be funny if you're now the one conforming—a traditional house in the suburbs or a three-bedroom apartment on the fourth floor of a stained, crumbling old building, three cute children, a cheating husband of your own. Would you even remember me?

*

The woman in black rests the yellow paperback on the rack, giving it a last caress with those long thin fingers. That book was responsible for some of my worst neuroses. It isn't worth reading again and risking the return of my old preoccupation with the Holocaust, the return of those claustrophobic nightmares. My life is so full of new obsessions, why invite the old ones back?

The woman raises her hand in a gesture that makes me weak at the knees. It's that flinging of a Tiger Lily braid off a shoulder, even so many years later and when the braid isn't there anymore and the once soft black hair has changed its texture and turned gray.

How do you approach a complete stranger and say, "Shalom, I'm Shelli"? What if she answered, "Shalom back to you, but who cares?"

I can't risk her indifference. But I must let her know who I am.

*

Rona hesitates. She should buy *Salamandra* for the sake of that long-lost friendship. No, she shouldn't. She drops it on the pile and strokes it with her fingertips, abandoned like Shelli. Discarded. In the time it takes her to hesitate more, *Salamandra* finds a new buyer. The platinum blonde with the pile of books, the serious reader, the kid in a candy store, makes room for another one.

As Rona mourns the lost book, that remnant of Shelli, she notices the hideous pewter ring on the other woman's finger.

*

I try trapping her attention by covering the yellow book with my left hand, spreading my palm wide across the cover. If she sees my ring, she'll immediately recognize me.

Won't she?

*

What's so hideous about that ring? Rona always pays attention to rings and hands. But what she usually does is about to change. From now on she'll notice other things, such as hair and clothes, mostly her own. I'm the new Rona, she decides, no more gray hair or black clothes for me. She looks down at her dress. She should buy something pink.

A Small Country about to Vanish

The woman with the lime-green carry-on luggage, the wearer of the ugly ring, stands transfixed. Stares at Rona.

This is the worst timing. Rona doesn't want some nudnik, who may know her from the supermarket, from Avivim, or from PTA meetings, to start asking stupid questions about where she's going and why. Rona turns her back on the woman and on the section of depressing Hebrew literature. She grabs a few romance novels randomly—*Love's Fire, Spring of Passion, Heart's Desire*, or whatever. Read one, read them all. The blonde with the ring stands like a statue, gaping at her, blocking her way to the counter. In a hurry, Rona brushes against her.

"Sliha," Rona says, immediately adding in English, "Excuse me." Because at the airport you never know what language to speak.

*

The spark passing between us translates into thousands of needles, taking me back in time to a school morning. The woman in black pays with a credit card and flees Steimatsky like a fugitive. She carries a blue purse, but no luggage.

A shrill alarm sounds. "Ma'am, you have to pay for the merchandise."

I look down. My intended purchases are still under my arm. I drop the books on the counter and start after her, dragging my luggage behind me.

"Hey," I call out.

It's like watching a movie when you cry out, "Turn around, he's behind you" or "Look up, she's in front of you," but you have no control over what happens.

The woman in black vanishes into the thickening airport crowd, out of my life.

Victoria Avilan

I buy *Salamandra* and read it cover to cover on the way to London. Indeed, it opens old wounds, brings back the old obsession, but not with the Holocaust. With Rona Lubliner and her long fingers.

A Small Country about to Vanish

23

Rona looks up at the departure screen. An El Al flight is scheduled to leave in a few hours for Los Angeles, which isn't that far from her destination, Acapulco, Mexico. From there she'll take another flight to Mexico, or she can stay at the Beverly Hills Hotel for a day or two. What's good for Harrison Ford is good enough for her. And Eithan is paying.

She stops at the ATM for cash, but realizes it will give out only shekels. She'll need American dollars. At the counter she uses her Visa for a one-way ticket to Los Angeles. Although Eithan's paying, Rona buys economy rather than business class. The new Rona wants to sit with, to mingle with, a wide variety of travelers.

The ticket agent eyes her suspiciously. "One way?"

"One way," she answers.

"I can't blame you," he says, more to himself than to her.

She stands in line for a passport check. How relaxed everything is. No stress. A burst of cheers comes from behind her.

"Goal!"

Her fellow passengers are watching a soccer game on a large screen. Israel has just scored against Brazil, and two little kids are jumping on top of their suitcases, cheering.

This airport is first on the hit lists of the world, yet there aren't any guns in sight. A skinny girl with pink fingernails and quick, clipped movements checks Rona's ticket and passport.

"One way?" she asks. "No luggage?" These two items would have raised a red flag in any other international airport, but not in Ben Gurion. Security checks don't bother with people like Rona who carry an Israeli passport, speak fluent Hebrew and are calm and composed. The girl hands Rona back her ticket and passport, saying, "Have a safe flight." Her courteous smile hides the fact that she's trained in contact combat and can kill a grown man, can easily crush his windpipe between two manicured fingers.

She isn't much older than my Gila, Rona thinks. And she looks less menacing.

I hope you also use condoms had been Rona's last maternal advice. Such angry words. Had she known that would be her last advice, Rona would've used a softer tone. She would've added, *I hope he treats you well. I hope you're his one and only, his Isolde.* She would have warned, *Don't accept candy and roses from a man, particularly not your husband.*

What a coward she is! Instead of clinging to her tough reality, remaining her children's source of strength and advice whether they want it or not, she's escaping. Running. Looking only forward and not back.

Let it go. You're not escaping your reality but rather being squeezed out of it like the ooze from an ugly pimple that sprouts on a bride's forehead on her wedding day.

Another passport check, another metal detector, and Rona is released into the terminal. And release is the operative word, describing what Rona feels as she exhales, liberating the tension from her body. She's learned to anticipate and enjoy the sudden loss of tension whenever she leaves her homeland.

And what does that say about her homeland?

The terminal is an international spot, a large shopping center, like Avivim. The only hints reminding Rona that she's still in her soon-to-be-abandoned country are the Hebrew signs above the stores and the flight announcements in all languages, including Hebrew.

A Small Country about to Vanish

She browses and chooses a red carry-on suitcase that will fit under her seat in economy. As she opens the case to gauge the space inside, she's pulled into darkness, gripped by sudden panic. Two forces with equal strength tear at her.

One force screams, *What are you doing? You have responsibilities, your mother needs you, your children, even Eithan.*

The other force calmly says, *You've done your best for them. They'll be alright.*

Her mother. Rona wonders if Eva, leaving Hungary in her twenties, had felt the same doubts Rona now feels. What was it like to leave everything familiar and make oneself homeless? Had Eva stored the piano in the ship's belly, or was it out in the common dining area? Was there a dining area? Was she asked to entertain the passengers with Beethoven's sonatas on their lengthy trip to Palestine?

She'd heard Eva talking about the trip, but those stories had skipped her mind. Skipped her heart as well. They had nothing to do with her, and they always ended sadly.

History repeats itself, Shelli had often said. Rona had never forgotten those words. And she believes Shelli's words. Eva's stories do belong to Rona, and in the most intimate sense. Both Shelli and Eva had been right.

Eva had left a world hostile to her kind. The place Rona is leaving is hostile but less discriminating. An exploding bomb accepts and welcomes all races and religions—Jews, Arabs, Christians, Buddhists.

Rona shakes off her thoughts and picks up more necessities.

Her suitcase is filling up nicely with essentials: cosmetics, toothbrush, a few pairs of CK underwear. Eva had her piano, her friends, her best friend Ruth, and a slim figure when she faced the unknown. Rona has none of those comforts. Well, she has a cellphone, credit cards, twenty-five years of experience on her mother, and chocolate.

Colorful packages wink at her from the counter. She caresses a blue package featuring a brown and white cow—Elite milk chocolate, smooth, no nuts or marzipan. It's her favorite, but what's the point in keeping the same eating habits when otherwise taking dramatic measures? She leaves the chocolate on the shelf and buys granola bars.

Is she ready? She doesn't feel ready. She feels . . . like she left something, many things, undone.

Had Eva left unfinished business? She'd been a pretty thing, barely older than Gila, when she'd abandoned her family to become its only survivor. Would Rona be . . . ?

No, don't even think about it. Let all such thoughts go to hell.

She remembers their relentless siding with their father against her, the birth control pills, the clicking red high heels in the toilet of a Mexican restaurant.

They all betrayed her.

24

When had Rona last seen the economy section of a 747? She pushes her way through the narrow aisle, locates her window seat and stows her luggage. Who would sit next to her? A talker? A cougher with smelly feet? A sniffer with no awareness of his bad habit? She can take anything—a scratcher, a constant talker—but please, not a sniffer, especially not the kind who drags it all the way up from his toes.

A baby's shriek pierces the air, followed by loud crying and a man's consoling voice. Rona turns around to see the source of her torment for the next twenty-four hours. The flight isn't really that long, but with a stop in Toronto and a crying baby behind her . . .

The baby's frightened little face is contorted and red, his or her lips trembling.

Instinctively Rona stretches out her arms, "Let me try."

The man, exasperated, gives her the baby.

Rona squeezes the crying baby tightly against her chest. She strokes the soft back slowly, gently. She senses the parade of passengers constantly moving down the aisle toward their seats. The faces of each of her loves click like a slide show behind her closed eyelids. The cheating Eithan, the fake-religious Tally—the most troubled ones first. Daniella, who denies her age, who tries to steal Gila. Gila, longing to be thin, longing for an acne-free forehead, longing for another mother. Mike, who prefers to play ball but agrees to play piano just for her. Did he manage that Scriabin without her cues from the first row? Did he wear the white shirt she'd ironed or the creased one? Could he tell the difference? Eva, who wants her murdered family back. Uri. What does Uri want?

Please forgive me, all of you. I didn't belong.

In a sea of nervous activity and sharp snaps of overhead compartments, Rona becomes a vessel of tranquility. She lets all the unwanted love she leaves behind pour into the crying, squirming baby. She pictures Mike, who is thoughtful and sensitive but who tries to be more like his rowdy friends by tattooing slogans on his shaved skull. She thinks of the precious twin boys staring up at the piano, their little fingers itching to play it.

All her loves have one connection in common: a longing for the verboten.

Now Rona is giving herself the gift of her own forbidden—freedom from her loved ones.

The tiny body of someone else's baby calms with each stroke of her hand. The infant still whimpers, but less vigorously. *What will become your verboten, little baby?* The answer is obvious: *whatever your daddy, the man sitting behind me, denies you most vehemently—religion, Ka-Tsetnik's novels, piano or tennis lessons—will become your strongest desire.*

Rona makes her breathing coincide with the baby's faster cycle until they fall into a rhythm, two of the baby's inhalations to one of hers.

Still no one sits next to her. Rona sticks her nose into the baby's dark, curly hair and inhales Johnson and Johnson's shampoo. She opens her eyes a crack and notices the pink collar of a bunny suit. A girl. She hugs her tighter, feeling the fragile bones of the soft back under her fingers, imagining that she's holding her namesake, Roni, Tally's little girl.

"You're wonderful," says the man, reaching for his daughter. "Thanks for making her sleep."

A Small Country about to Vanish

She wants to hold her longer, smell that shampoo, enjoy that calmness.

"Any time." Reluctantly, Rona hands back the sleeping baby.

"Hi," says a cheerful voice. A young woman in a denim jacket takes the seat next to Rona. "I'm Thalma, who are you?" she asks in English, kicking a well-worn gray backpack underneath the seat in front of her.

"I'm Rona."

"Nice to meet you." She shakes the hand Rona offers. "I don't want to leave. This country is so insane and fun . . ."

She has a slight lisp, a slur, as if her tongue is too lazy to move in her mouth.

"Insane, right," Rona says. "Are you a tourist?"

"Not exactly," she says. "Mom was born here. We were traveling together and now we had to separate and I got upset. That's why my eyes are so red. Look." She opens her eyes widely at Rona, who sees the tears and some redness she'd attribute to the excessive use of the woman's now-running mascara. She also spots a gold ring on the tip of her tongue, the reason for her lisp.

A constant talker, Rona identifies her seatmate. Does she sniff as well?

By now all the passengers have settled into their seats, like eggs into their egg-crate protection, and the flight attendants are preparing for takeoff.

Panic engulfs Rona. She unclasps her seat belt, needing to get up and demand, *Let me out*. To declare, *I'm an impostor, not a passenger at all*.

"Seat belt, please," says a passing male flight attendant. This crisp, no-bullshit command, as well as Rona's inherent good manners, stops her from throwing herself against the exit door.

You only get to escape once a day, she tells herself.

Next to her, the woman has been talking in a normal voice, unaware of Rona's sudden distress. Rona doesn't know what she's been saying, but the slow American voice does for her what, only moments ago, she had done for the crying baby. The voice relaxes her into the chosen, now inevitable, fate. Destination: Los Angeles.

"I'm sorry, what's your name again?" Rona asks.

"It's Thalma, but Mom sometimes calls me Tally."

A pang of pain hits Rona between the eyes. How different she is from her own uptight Tally.

"You can call me Tally if you want. Actually, you remind me of Mom."

"I like Thalma," Rona says. Somehow Tally doesn't suit this charming, outgoing friendliness.

Rona is jealous, envious of the closeness this young woman feels for her mother, the way she talks about her with sentimentality and affection. Rona has never felt such devotion from her own children or toward Eva. She'd like to meet the mother who's so worthy of this affection, since one gets as good as one is capable of giving.

I failed at giving.

The aircraft is finally in the air. Rona sees the city lights. Tel Aviv with its small, serpentine streets is just as dense from above. As dense and as messy as the lives it contains.

She turns to Thalma. "Why aren't you and your mom flying together?"

"I have an audition and Mom has a quick meeting in London with her publisher."

As Thalma wipes her wet eyes with a tissue, Rona sees the pewter ring on her finger. Her heart quickens.

"I like your ring," she says. Not because it is true, but as a conversation hook.

A Small Country about to Vanish

"This is Mom's good luck ring. She never takes it off, but she gave it to me for my audition—"

"I need some good luck myself." Rona's hand trembles as she reaches for the ring. "May I see it, please?"

Thalma slips it off her finger, generous and eager to share her luck. Rona holds her breath when she examines the cheap ring. The warrior maiden, like the one she once owned and had named the Valkyrie. There are thousands of such rings on people's fingers.

Metal belts click as impatient passengers start to get up, ignoring the fasten-seat-belt signs. Thalma/Tally—who so far hasn't sniffed or scratched or coughed even once, to Rona's relief—keeps talking in that slow, relaxed voice.

"I had such fun in Tel Aviv. The nightclubs, the restaurants, the beach. I'm going to visit more often. It was a blast. Oops, I really shouldn't use that word, should I?"

Rona clenches the ring inside her tight fist, asking a cold object to disclose the truth. But what truth does she want from it? It's just an ugly pewter ring, one of thousands, millions. Hadn't she just seen a similar ring on someone's finger at the bookstore?

"Were you afraid?" she asks.

"Aren't you afraid every day? You guys have such courage."

"Where there's no choice, there's no courage," Rona says.

She expects an argument, forgetting she's not in her living room, where Asher, Eithan and Daniella try talking her out of any idea, even when they agree with her. Thalma only smiles in acceptance.

Rona feels like she should play hostess. As she can't provide more exciting refreshments—a chocolate cake, Turkish coffee, shish kabob—she offers her new friend a package of crackers, which Thalma accepts with gratitude.

Rona hands her back the ring. "Tell me about your mom."

Thalma munches on a cracker. "What do you want to know?"

"Everything," Rona says.

"Gawd, how you remind me of her. Where should I start? Mom loves to play games. She has this game she started when Erik and I were little. She'd invent dangerous situations and ask, *How would you save yourselves*? She wanted to teach us self-preservation. She has this obsession with history repeating itself and knowing how to recognize signs of trouble. She writes."

"Your mother writes?"

"That's what she does for a living. What am I saying? She more like lives in her own stories as she writes them. We all tease her about it." Thalma smiles. "Mom used to make-believe she could play the piano—she has a real antique one that's worth a lot of money. She'd put on a CD, sit by the piano and pretend to play Rachmaninoff or Chopin for me and my brother and our friends. It was funny because she'd yell, *staccato*, *legato*, like some crazy piano teacher or conductor. She'd make funny faces, like this."

Thalma elongates her face in an expression of exaggerated importance.

Thalma laughs out loud at the memory, but Rona is again washed with doubts. Such coincidences don't belong in real life. She tears her gaze from Thalma's mirthful face and stares down at her hands, the way she does after playing a favorite sonata. She stretches her thin fingers, thinking sadly, *Long and thin, the way the rest of me used to be when everyone liked me. When I liked myself.*

"—Mom would pretend to be playing in Carnegie Hall. It was always her dream, but she never learned to play."

"Why?" Rona asks.

"When she wanted to start, she was already too old."

A Small Country about to Vanish

This advice sounds vaguely familiar to Rona. Vaguely dangerous.

"That's silly," she says. "There's nothing such as too old if you have a dream."

"That's what I tell her."

"Now, Thalma, what do you do?"

She works as a waitress at a diner.

"But I'm really an actress, waiting to be discovered. Casting directors come to eat there all the time. People say I look like Sharon Stone in *Basic Instinct*." She takes a drag of an imaginary cigarette and crosses her slim legs a la Stone. "What do you think?"

"If this is up to me, you're hired," Rona says, unsure of the grammar in a language she isn't used to speaking.

She has nothing to lose by saying it. With that burned, oxidized hair and the raccoon-black eyeliner, Thalma reminds Rona not of Sharon Stone in her glory, but rather of the unlucky Diane, the loser wannabe actress from that David Lynch film. Thalma is about thirty but looks younger because of her marvelous figure, that hopeless optimism and what Gila would call inner immaturity.

As if to reinforce that image, Thalma says, "Mom and I live in a fabulous place by the beach. I'm a Pisces, you see, moon rising in Aquarius. A fortune teller once told me I should always live by the water—"

Rona feels exhausted, bored with horoscopes. She dozes off. When she opens her eyes, the seat next to her is vacant. Had the conversation been a dream? That stranger—whose Israeli-born mother wears a pewter ring and loves to make up stories—that woman/girl who isn't seated next to her anymore, seems unreal and too good to be true.

Rona longs for Thalma, the daughter she would have liked to have. Was Thalma another angel escorting her onto the next world, pretending to be a fellow passenger as Gibril pretended to be a cab driver?

The aircraft is dark, all the shades are drawn, and she can hear light snoring behind her and the even drone of the engines. Was the baby real? She hadn't heard her cry or make a sound since she'd put her to sleep. Rona wants to turn around and validate the baby's existence, see her again, but a chill goes through her body and she dreads finding out.

Most of the passengers are asleep, though some pace restlessly, stretching their legs. Sudden turbulence makes her shiver. She opens the window shade a crack, and sharp light floods in. Directly below she sees what she had seen on many previous flights, the black and white terrain of Greenland, the wrong place for crashing. Rona sighs. How cold it seems, like the unknown world she's about to face all alone.

And the seat next to her remains empty.

Thalma, then, had been a dream, an apparition. How nice it would've been to have really made a friend.

The aroma of freshly brewed coffee tickles her nostrils, bringing back the feel of a normal morning. Only yesterday she and Jihan had sat at the kitchen counter sipping their first cup of Turkish coffee before starting their cleaning routine, and now she is somewhere else, and the dishes she left in the sink are someone else's problem.

"Good morning," says a slow, familiar voice. "How do you take it?"

Rona looks up with relief. A smiling Thalma is holding two Styrofoam cups.

"Cream and sugar? I even found some cookies in the galley."

"Just black for me please." The new Rona takes her coffee like the thin Daniella does. "No cookies, thanks."

A Small Country about to Vanish

Thalma unclasps Rona's tray and rests the cup in front of her. "Café Botz," she says. "That's how Mom likes it. Mud thick." She settles in. "Oh, I can't wait to see my sweet Harley."

"Your boyfriend? Your dog? Your kid?" Rona sips, and the hot bitterness wakes her up.

Thalma laughs. "My Harley Davidson."

Thalma describes the fully accessorized motorcycle she'd bought second hand, telling how she polishes it and zips with her biker buddies up and down the Malibu canyons. It has chrome covers, decorative accents, a red tank bra. Rona's head spins. Such excitement and enthusiasm about a piece of metal!

More turbulence shakes the plane. Thalma switches to the previous subject: her hopes for a future in television or movies. She sometimes volunteers at a nonprofit organization and helps during public events.

"I got to be a seat filler at the Oscars last year. I sat next to Jack Nicholson. What a nice guy."

Rona listens, amazed at this telling of an entire life story to a stranger just because they're sitting together on a near-twenty-hour-long flight.

She wants to hear more about Thalma's mother, but Thalma keeps drifting away on various tangents about herself. Rona finds this girl/woman fascinating, not because of her great intelligence, but because that fervor is as refreshing and intoxicating as a cold beer on a summer day. Both Gila and Mike, still in their teens, have more maturity than Thalma. Yet there's something sweet in her innocence. She's someone you want to take home with you and protect, because you know that eventually she'll get very hurt.

Take home? What home? Rona is homeless now. She has nothing but a lot of credit, spread lavishly, like butter, across the bread of five major credit cards. She knows she can be traced this way, but why should she care? Her only crime is buying time away from those who betrayed her. Let them realize she hasn't come home, worry a little, learn to live without her.

Breakfast is served. Thalma eats everything off her tray, praising the omelet, the yogurt, the quality of the cookies. Rona can't ingest anything but coffee; the sight of food makes her sick. She's a new woman who lost her appetite and is about to give away all her secrets to a total stranger from California.

Intrigued by this American openness, Rona wants to take it for a test drive.

"Coffee? Tea?" asks the effeminate flight attendant, cocking one hip as he holds the edge of the beverage cart.

"Coffee, please." Rona sets the plastic cup on the tray for a refill and without looking at Thalma, says, "I left my husband and my family."

25

Thalma squeals in amazement. "Do you have a lover?"

"Me? A lover?" Rona laughs. "With this figure?"

Rona stares down at what she considers to be the least attractive package of human flesh she knows. She ridicules Thalma's blunder, but she's flattered just the same. She needs that flattery and she tells everything without censorship. What ease, how comforting to tell all to a stranger she'll never see again, someone who won't judge her, not even for her ugly broken English.

For the first time in her life, Rona articulates her fears, hopes and wants to another human being who actually listens with fascination, the way her family and friends never have.

Any conversation with Daniella, for instance, had ulterior motives, competition, and overblown comparisons of achievements. Daniella would remind Rona of the past, would make digs such as *We always thought* you'd *be the one*. She'd have enough finesse not to elaborate, but Rona could extrapolate the unspoken words. *We thought you'd be the one to make it big, and look, I'm the famous artist and there are all our friends who made it and are playing music in Europe and here you are fat, forty-something, forgotten*.

Thalma seems mesmerized by Rona's story. Done cleaning off her own tray, she starts picking at Rona's untouched food. She reacts often and appropriately. "Really, red lipstick?" "The ladies room? No shit." Some of her exclamations are new to Rona, but she understands the spirit. She is being admired.

Then Thalma tops it all by asking, "Would you let me play you in a movie?"

It would be a total miscast, but the chance of such a film being made is equal to the chance of Thalma starring in it. Those close to her always want something from Rona and here's this generous woman—girl, really—who thinks that Rona's life is interesting enough for a movie, and what's more, she wants to play her!

Rona catches a glimpse of the praying Orthodox men in black holding a minyan in the clearing by the exit doors. "Sure, Tally," she says, calling her that because those men swaying back and forth remind her of Moishe, her pious son-in-law.

"You are so like Mom," Thalma says again. "The way you just called me Tally and looked so lost."

By the time they land for refueling in Toronto, Rona has a true, new friend.

*

Eithan stays up all night. Old Max is warming his feet, sleeping as usual. The house has emptied of most people and those who stayed, friends of Mike and Gila, are draped on chairs and carpets and on couches and in the spare bedrooms. The sounds of light snoring fill the huge living room.

He keeps staring at the door, wide awake, waiting for Rona. The lyrics of a song keep singing themselves on a loop, taking permanent residence in his body and mind. *Our hope is not yet lost, the hope of two thousand years . . . Hatikva*, the national anthem—sung in reverence at national events, sung with twisted lyrics by mischievous school children—now chants from his lips like a mantra.

*

A Small Country about to Vanish

While waiting in the secure holding area, the passengers help themselves to refreshments, courtesy of the Toronto airport. Thalma has a pastry. Rona, who still can't eat, is content with black coffee and water. Some of the passengers are sprawled on the carpeted floor, snoozing, using their bags as pillows. It is night in their place of origin and they are tired. One woman is twisted like a pretzel in a complex yoga pose. The minyan has gathered again, men in black facing eastward toward Jerusalem, swaying and praying.

Thalma is slumped in the chair next to Rona, head back, long, thin legs stretched a mile in front of her. Rona recalls a time when she could slump that way without looking like a fat old slob. She sits upright, dignified, holding a bottle of water.

"Do you have a place to stay?" Thalma asks.

"The Beverly Hills Hotel. Eithan is paying."

"No fucking way. You'll stay with Mom and me. We've been looking for a new roommate since the last guy left, so the guestroom is ready. We were so happy to see him go. He paid the rent, but he used to play the guitar all night and sing in a falsetto."

"Won't your mother mind?"

"Not at all. Mom gets back from London tomorrow. She'll be happy to meet you. She's used to me bringing people home —"

Thalma's mom is like Rona, whose house is always full of kids, friends of her very popular children. She'd open Mike's door at night and find three of his friends in sleeping bags on the floor. The same with Gila. Lately she's became more strict with both her kids, her children who aren't children anymore.

Again Rona winces at the memory of that last argument about those birth control pills. The old Rona felt cheated and angry. The new Rona may have said the same thing, "I hope you also use condoms," but with a light-hearted attitude, disarming, like Daniella.

What a nightmare she must have been, and now she understands. Rona's hand is on her cellphone. She is about to call and apologize to all of them for having been a tyrant. She'll turn around and get on the next flight back to Israel.

Gila, Mike and Tally all deserve an apology for the tough childhood she's given them. Those four-to-six piano hours must have been hell to have pushed Tally into religion. Even Eithan deserves an apology. Especially Eithan, whom she'd pushed into the arms of a worthless floozy with cheap lipstick that smears . . .

What have I done?

Thalma's calm and slow voice lands Rona back in her new life. "—Mom calls them Thalma's strays. No fucking way you're going to a hotel."

I'm a stray. Rona drops the phone back into her purse and smiles, adding a new English expression to her growing vocabulary: *no fucking way*.

A Small Country about to Vanish

26

Rona wipes the steam off the mirror and dries herself with a fluffy pink towel. A total stranger with a swollen face and faded freckles stares back at her. In the cabinet underneath the sink she finds everything a visitor could need—more clean towels, toothpaste, soaps and shampoos—as if they were expecting her. She hears a toilet flushing, the shower on the floor above.

She slips naked between the cool sheets on the queen-size bed. Through the open window of the basement room she hears the world's shoes. Running feet in flip flops. Women in high heels, or maybe men. Anything is possible here in Los Angeles.

A knock on the door and Thalma pokes her smiling face in, hair wrapped in a towel turban. "You need anything?"

"No, thank you," Rona says, sleepy.

"Later I'll go get some groceries. There's nothing but booze in the fridge. Sleep tight."

They'd stopped at a drive-thru on the way from the airport, but Rona had been too tired, and her stomach too queasy, to eat the mass-produced mess that Thalma had stuffed down.

The glacier-speed of the custom lines had been grueling, and the wait for Thalma's luggage, the shuttle ride to the parking lot where her car was parked, and then getting out of the airport and to Thalma's house had been an ordeal because it was rush hour and traffic hadn't moved.

Now that she's finally clean, Rona is ready to be alone and to sleep.

The bed is so very soft, too soft and warm, like a fluffy cloud. Rona's own bed, the one she's abandoned, is Spartan-hard by comparison. Here people spoil themselves with little luxuries, expect more from life than mere day-to-day survival. She keeps her eyes open, beyond tired in a place where fatigue has spun itself into delirium.

Here she goes again, giving herself another cultural lecture instead of falling asleep.

The clock's digital display says it's almost noon. Ten p.m. in Tel Aviv. What are they doing without her? Thoughts dart through her groggy mind.

Thalma's mom will arrive from London tomorrow—or is today already tomorrow?

Who is Thalma's mom, the woman who pretends to play the piano, who makes up stories, who wears a pewter ring, the warrior maiden? Would she mind an unexpected guest?

Has Rona made the right decision or a colossal mistake?

Sleep now, worry later.

Of course she'll pay them rent. Rona has wads of dollars, money she withdrew against her credit cards. Eithan's credit cards. He'll trace her as soon as the bills come in, but she doesn't mind. For once in her life she's escaping a problem rather than solving it.

A familiar rolling sound fills the street—a skateboard racing down the slope. She smells geranium, the fragrance of home, and thinks again, *I made myself homeless.*

"Hey, dude," yells a girl outside her window.

"Hey," a boy answers. "Did you catch big waves today?"

She hears bursts of laughter and conversation, and more skateboards rolling down the steep alley. A squeal, a scrape, even more laughter as someone falls but doesn't get hurt, or pretends not to be hurt out of pride. Later he or she will be black and blue. Those sounds and smells are like home, only in

A Small Country about to Vanish

English. People want the same wherever they are: pride, big waves, food, love, sex. A roof over their heads.

They also want peace, *shalom*, but they don't know they want it until they lose it. If this were Israel, shalom would be first on every wish list.

Hey, dude in English. *Shalom aleichem* in Hebrew. *Salam aleikum* in Arabic. Both Hebrew and Arabic mean the same, *may peace be on you*.

The kids outside this particular window don't wish each other peace. They enjoy skateboarding as much as her Mike does, but unlike Mike, they take peace for granted because they live in the serene dreamland of Marcia Brady.

Finally her exhausted body conquers her restless mind. The foreign feeling of peace acts like a powerful cocktail, lulling her to sleep.

*

Startled, Gila wakes up. The blue cast of the moon shines through her window. She opens her eyes with difficulty—they're swollen. Crickets are chirping, and the scent of night flowers floats through the air. At the sound of snoring next to her, she turns to look.

Sophie and Ramón. What are they doing at the foot of her bed, curled into each other like two sleeping dogs or, rather, like twins in the womb? Sophie is in a white tank top and her favorite tattered jeans, worn at the knees. Ramón is wearing his new, dark denims and is naked from the waist up.

What will Ima, with all her old-fashioned hang-ups, say when she sees them?

A blow hits her; Ima is dead. She died last night in the pigua.

Gila starts crying. As she washes down a little white pill with the lukewarm water from the bottle of Mey Eden—Water of Paradise, what a fucking joke; this is hell—Gila recalls her mother's expression when she held the pills. It was more pain than anger, as if Gila had betrayed her. Now she's sure, in spite of her inhibitions, that Ima could've helped her with this problem, a much bigger problem than that stupid field trip to Poland they fought so bitterly over. Much bigger than simple birth control.

The truth—Gila doesn't take Estrostep to prevent pregnancy. That's *not* Gila's problem. Dr. Rosenblatt, Daniella's gynecologist, had only prescribed the medication for her acne.

Gila is desperate for her mother, needs her now more than ever.

The truth isn't something she could ever confess to Daniella or even to her father. Only her mother would understand. Only Ima would know what to do.

Gila is torn inside, in love with two. Both her loves know about it, accept it, even tease each other about it.

Look at them now, sleeping together, Ramón's mouth slightly open and Sophie's face buried in his shoulder. Sophie even suggested that they live together, form an alternative family like in that French film they watched with the totally hot Victoria Abril. Because why can't you love two people, Sophie wanted to know.

Gila knows you can't do it, can't always love one, much less two at the same time. She'll have to choose.

But pregnancy prevention? Ridiculous.

Gila plays with Ramón, yes, but she's only ever gone all the way—and only for the first time a couple of days ago—with Sophie.

27

She opens her eyes to the sound of screeching tires. Where is she? How long has she slept? Rona's mouth feels so dry, she's dying for a cold and fizzy drink. Her gaze sweeps along the walls of the dusky room. The red digital display of the clock says 5:15 p.m. She slept for five hours.

A door is open to the adjacent bathroom. A television is balanced on a wooden chest of drawers, a Mac laptop sits on a desk, its screen saver in motion—a Harley Davidson with smaller motorcycles spinning around it like moons around a planet. Thalma's computer.

The metal ceiling fan above her head is at rest, resembling sharp knives.

There's just enough light to identify the poster on the opposite wall—Edward Hopper's *Chop Suey*. Rona loves this painting with its two women in matching hats immersed in conversation and washed by light from the window at a Chinese restaurant. A green table lamp has been moved to the windowsill to allow them an unobstructed view of each other. Do they meet every day, or are they catching up after many years? What secrets are they disclosing, what news, happy or sad? Despite each other's company, they both seem lonely. And the pale-faced woman in the green dress, has she caught her husband with his pants down and his dick smeared with red lipstick?

No, I'm the one! Rona chokes out a cry at the full realization of what she's done.

She recalls the jagged line of events that brought her here: being sick in the ladies room; coming face to face with the guilty Eithan; the cab and its driver; the airport; the bookstore and that yellow book, *Salamandra*; the flight and sweet Thalma, an American stranger who has opened her heart and home to Rona.

I'm crazy, what have I done? She sits up in bed and rubs her eyes, something Daniella keeps warning her not to do. "It gives you bags under your eyes."

Her children and her mother deserve to know where she is. Poor Eva has already lost so much. She instinctively reaches for the cellphone in her purse, turns it on and waits for the Nokia logo to appear. When it does, she dials her home number. Instead of ringing, a recording of a male voice says, "Your international call cannot be completed as dialed." She tries again, adding the country code. Now a Hebrew recording of a female voice says that something has to be activated.

She eyes the house phone on her bed stand; it's there for her, but it isn't the same. Without her cellphone, Rona feels stranded and lost. How dependent we are on our cells of communication, she thinks. In her dangerous country the cellphone is sacred. It allows the talkative, nomadic Jew to keep yacking while on the move.

What if I'm a ghost, unable to communicate with my loved ones? Rona's chest tightens with anxiety. What if the state of death just means spending eternity in the eeriness of this dark basement room, thirsty, with Hopper's *Chop Suey* reflecting her endless loneliness? Again, she expects God or his angel to meet her at the gate of heaven, like in the jokes, and ask three questions or give her two choices.

Silly me, of course I'm alive.

Rona picks up the receiver on the night stand, dials her home number and hangs up before the first ring. She can't stand the thought of hearing Eithan's voice, or Gila's, for that matter. Not when Gila hasn't talked to her for the last week.

The computer. She'll email them and get it over with. The slate floor under her bare feet sends chills through her nakedness. Rona puts on her new pink track suit. It needs a few washes to lose its rough texture. Sitting at the computer, she stubs her big toe on the wooden desk. "Kus Emak!" The Arabic expletive escapes her mouth.

She clicks the Internet Explorer icon. No doubt the generous Thalma won't mind her using it. She types in Eithan's email address.

The subject? Rona.

How odd to communicate with Eithan in English. This fact alone will feel like a note from the beyond to him.

The credit cards are overdrawn, but don't cancel them. Let's call it an even swap. I'm giving you your freedom and taking my own. Tell Ima and the kids that I love them and not to look for me. I'm not angry at you, although I was. You are still the love of my life, but it's my turn to live a little. Do Svidaniya.

She hesitates, about to change the greeting to *goodbye* or simply *shalom*. Why make it seem as if the incident in the ladies room was the sole reason for her actions? It was merely the final straw. She leaves *do svidaniya* and hits Send. The Russian woman was the catalyst and now she and Rona share a strange sisterhood: women who will have to survive Eithan Rosenthal.

Eithan can hit Reply and write back, but she'll ignore it, delete it.

Now for that cold drink . . .

Since throwing up in Avivim, Rona hasn't eaten much. Only a few peanuts on the flight and enough coffee to fill a small bathtub. Her appetite has died. When she climbs the wooden stairs, she stops. Not only to catch her breath, but to browse the books piled on the shelves above the stairs and on the stairs themselves. Thalma and her mother have run out of space for their books.

Almost immediately she finds the shelves of Hebrew books. Etgar Keret, Agnon, Amos Oz. *Ka-Tsetnik*? Rona gasps in dread. Either she is walking through a dream—a nightmare—or this is indeed the state of death, of neither here nor there. What if this is her personal Judgment Day and she is about to pay for sins she committed in the past? What if all those religious fanatics were right and she was wrong?

"You don't really believe this shit, do you?" she whispers to herself.

She stops browsing and slowly climbs to the second floor. The house is silent, but she hears traffic and voices from the street. Where is Thalma? Thalma's mother? A front door of thick, textured glass appears to her right. More books line the way up to the third floor. She goes up. On the third floor, a kitchen opens on her left and on her right, a great room furnished in earth colors, a shaggy, white rug on bamboo floors and more shelves bursting with books. How wonderful. How different from her own pretentious home designed by professionals. This beauty is natural, letting in the red, purple and orange of the sunset through the glass walls, the tranquil Pacific Ocean and in it, a cluster of white sails.

Rona tears her gaze from the sunset and opens the stainless steel refrigerator. Her hand gets glued to the tacky handle. This wouldn't happen in her home. She makes sure to wipe all door handles from sticky little fingers.

As Thalma has promised, the fridge is packed with beers, other bottles of alcohol, and not much food except for moldy leftovers in plastic containers. In the bottom drawer she finds a six-pack of Diet Coke and pops one open.

She studies the room.

Family photographs are scattered on the walls and on wooden surfaces. A little girl—Thalma—holding the hand of a dark man, probably her father. Thalma hasn't changed much. A blurred photo of a couple with two small children. A wedding photo on top of the piano, lit to a high gloss by the angle of the sun. About to pick up the photo, Rona stops dead.

Erard, Paris in that very ornamented, very familiar font is staring back at her.

Rona laughs out loud. So few of them are left in the world, yet they manage to find her. She opens the cover and touches the keyboard. She runs one hand through a few scales while standing, an old habit. What a cacophony! So out of tune.

She expects clouds of dust to move up in billows from each key, but she's wrong about that. No one plays this piano, but clean it is. She sits down and without hesitation starts playing the piece that makes any room in any land feel like home.

28

My flight back to Los Angeles was long and tiring, and I'm looking forward to a glass of Cabernet with my girl. She'd been smart to fly directly home from Tel Aviv since I had no time in London to see more than the inside of an office. I can't wait to tell her all about the contract for my short story collection.

When I get out of the cab I hear piano music echoing in the alley. This happens frequently. Every now and then I hear the piano welcoming me home, but when I go up to the living room, the music stops and the room is empty save for ghosts and memories.

Still, someone is playing scales with the rich resonance of a Bach étude. Either it's my imagination again, or Thalma has learned to play overnight. Maybe one of her Hells Angels buddies is the one playing. I shiver. Such moments bring back that yellowing ad in my purse. That's exactly how Rona used to play the scales when she wasn't busy arguing with Eva.

I carry my suitcase up the few stairs to the front door. *Clank, clank, clank.* When I'm tired, its lime green gives me a headache. At other times, I find the wild color useful, invigorating.

The suitcase is heavy, packed mostly with Hebrew books from Israel. The door is unlocked again. Thalma should be more careful. The neighborhood has had a lot of break-ins lately, what with the pier and the bars and the drunks going up and down the alley all day and night.

The music doesn't stop when I open the door, but gets louder. I leave my suitcase in the corner by the bedroom and stand listening. The soothing first notes of "The Moonlight Sonata." I smile to myself. Unless Thalma convinced a friend to serenade me on my arrival, I'm obviously suffering an early case of jet lag. Instead of rushing upstairs, I sigh with contentment and enjoy the music.

I remain leaning against the bookcase in the hallway, afraid that movement will wake me from my blessed state.

I close my eyes. How our past desires haunt us, as do our unexplained fears. We have a recurrent nightmare of suffocation and we don't know why. We buy a piano, although we'll never learn to play it. I live my life as a grownup, but my childhood's longings still rule, still take me to that extraordinary place my kids and friends named "Planet Shelli." Deep inside I've remained the girl who wanted to play the piano, who's had a one-sided love affair with it as sorrowful as the love I'd once had for a young woman ultimately unavailable to me.

The adagio sostenuto always reminded me of the Hungarian language—slow, profound, dark. Reminded me of the always-scrubbing Eva who shouted musical directions at her daughter. The pauses, the style, take me back to the time I lived vicariously through Rona Lubliner's fingertips.

I touch my cheeks. They're wet. I pause a little longer, extending the fantasy. It doesn't end. Here comes the *allegretto*.

Now curious even more than delighted, I kick off my shoes and mount the stairs to my living room. There I stop dead.

A full-figured woman with short gray hair sits at the piano, her back to me. The price tag is still attached and hanging from the collar of her shocking pink sweat suit. My auditory fantasies have turned visual. I sit quietly behind her, close my eyes again and listen. The short allegretto ends. Then the presto agitato.

I don't want her to stop. My old friend used to claim that interrupting the music kills the dead composer all over again.

As the last notes of the presto drift away, I open my eyes and watch the woman stare down to the keyboard and then lift each of her fingers, as if seeing her own hands for the first time.

No one else . . . Could it be?

"Oh, my . . ." I choke up.

She turns.

*

With her mind enveloped in the music, Rona examines her fingernails—a peculiarity she retains from an early age, a necessary transition from the dreamy world of Beethoven to the harsh reality of family arguments and political discussions. Over the years her palms grew larger, her fingers lengthened, and then she started wearing nail polish. In her rebellious stage she'd let her fingernails grow long—for the same reason she bought *Tristan ünd Isolde*—to spite Eva.

Rona hears a choked whisper.

She tears her gaze away from her hands and swivels around to face a slim, pale, older version of Thalma. The woman is staring at her.

"Good evening," Rona says.

*

Her crackly voice hasn't changed. I want to say, I know who you are. You're the girl who haunted me. The one who brushed against me, created sparks strong enough to set a fire, and then disappeared into the high school crowd, the airport crowd.

I have so much to say, but my throat is a thin straw. I have to draw small breaths so I won't black out.

She takes a long moment to recognize me. Like her, I've also changed. My hair is now platinum, I lost thirty-five pounds and gained the same in years.

*

I know this stranger.

Then the truth descends on Rona. None of what she's seen and done the past day was coincidence.

"Shelli," she says.

The woman nods, obviously unable to speak. Rona expects to be kicked out of the house for old time's sake, but Shelli does something odd and wholly unexpected.

*

Rona's hands are both in mine. I kiss each long finger—something I always wanted to do when the music ended—and she lets me. My breathing eases, as if those small kisses are gulps of oxygen. Would she shake me off? Would she say, "Sliha, excuse me," and again brush against me and out of my life?

Suddenly her whole body in the pink track suit trembles—the laughter of ridicule. So nothing has changed.

Yet when I look up, I see that she's not laughing, but is trying rather unsuccessfully to contain her sobs.

"It's you," she whispers.

The freckles around her nose and cheeks have faded and turned to age spots, but her eyes are the same sparkling violet-blue. Her arms enclose me and all the wasted years drop away.

*

Rona remembers the yellow circle of light on the ceiling above the macramé lamp and the crooning of Roussos. She also remembers the harsh "Liebestod." Her love for Shelli had been like Wagner, exciting because it was verboten. That day, both the soft song and the harsh one had played in her head, two different soundtracks, one desire, the other guilt. Rona had wanted both Eithan and Shelli, her boy-lover, who was absent, and her girl-lover, who had been present and whispering, "Yes, here."

Shelli had been shy at first, then demanding, directing. Rona had become freshly fascinated with her own hands, at how well they played that newness, that softness, that warmth. Her hands knew the correct fingering and positioning without instructions. No one yelled at her and demanded that she practice from four to six. *That* act of love came naturally. She was playing the violin, the cello, the entire orchestra, in legato, legatissimo and molto vibrato. At last, down on her knees, she'd put her mouth on that versatile new instrument. Until the gasp came.

The gasp hadn't been hers, hadn't been Shelli's. Suddenly her boy-lover towered over them, pain in his eyes. Next, Gidi Ishbitzky and Asher Schwartz leered down at them with that expression Rona would see on their faces for months, for years, afterward, when no one else cared to mention that horrible incident anymore. She'd overhear them bragging to their friends—the all-powerful hev're—how they'd caught Rona and Shelli, *you know, doing it*. Their words and their invasion turned her love for Shelli into something dirty and disgusting that she'd needed to forget.

A Small Country about to Vanish

Rona—the taste of Shelli still sweet in her mouth—had seized a random piece of clothing from the floor. Just as randomly she grabbed the first excuse that came to mind.

"I was just practicing," she lied to the speechless Eithan, "so I can do it with you."

Shelli covered herself with Rona's faded-into-pink dress. "You weren't just practicing," she said. "You liked it when I did the same to you."

Rona could never forgive her that truth.

How did they all get in, anyway, when she'd locked the front door? Or had she? After all these years, that invasion still felt like the memory of a rape.

*

"Your pink dress is here, somewhere," I say.

"You don't suppose I'd fit into it, do you?" Rona asks, pointing down at her crumpled track suit. "I'm into pink again."

"Very, very pink," I say.

"I have two more in very green and very turquoise."

"In the bookstore you were all in black."

"That Rona-in-black is dead."

"You were hugging a yellow book."

"*Salamandra*," she says. "I wish I'd bought it."

"You can have my copy," I say, "but I have to warn you—"

"Not a lot of laughs, eh?" Rona asks, half-smiling. "But you're a woman with a lime-green suitcase."

"Never yet missed it on a luggage carousel."

Rona points at the piano. "That thing needs serious tuning."

"It had plenty," I say. "Here, let me show you."

We get down on our aging knees and stick our heads into the belly of the piano—our comfort zone when we were girls. There we'd practiced our first kiss. I shine a flashlight inside and show Rona the signatures of all the tuners from the nineteenth century on.

"Is Eva still alive?" I ask.

"Yes," Rona says, "but she calmed down and I turned into her."

"Do you yell at your kids when they play piano?"

"All the time," she says. "I caused my oldest such trauma she turned to religion."

"What?" I ask, "she found Jesus?"

At that, Rona totally loses it, and the sound of her rolling laugh echoes hollow inside the dark piano.

"Sometimes I wish it were Jesus," she says, "but there's no compassion involved, just fanaticism."

Next she tells me about Eithan and Tally, Gila and Daniella, who have all failed her. "My life turned to shit." She talks about what brought her to this state of being homeless.

"My home and my piano are yours," I say.

"This sounds like an echo from the past," Rona says. Then, "I used to be so jealous of you."

This takes me by surprise. "You, of me?"

Rona lists the reasons. "Your mother wasn't bitter like mine, she was such a cool sabre who spoke Hebrew right and she didn't force you to play the piano. I was jealous because you were so sheltered and grounded in your family and your country."

"But now I'm the one floating, when you at least tried to make it work."

Rona shakes her head. "I failed my country, my husband, my children."

"I'm not exactly a success," I say, "although my son's going to be a lawyer."

"Good. I may need one." She adds softly, "I also failed as a friend."

"You have a chance to correct the friend fuck-up," I say.

I go for another round, shining the flashlight on signature after signature of the long-dead tuners. The light hits her swollen face and she doesn't seem real. This moment doesn't seem real. Eventually tired from all the talking and the excitement, we both doze off by the piano on the floor cushions.

"Mom, you're back!" Thalma cries out, waking me.

Sitting up, I'm about to introduce my oldest friend to my daughter, but Rona is gone and I'm facing Thalma by myself. I don't say anything. Thalma already thinks me weird.

Thalma stands akimbo over me, all geared up with leather and jeans, a nose ring, pierced eyebrow and full make-up. Impatient honking sounds from outside, followed by multiple beeps from her buddies, all those Hells Angels waiting for her to come out and play. Which means, in their world, *Get on your bike and let's go to the canyons*.

Thalma stares at me, eyes narrowed, mouth tight—her worried-daughter expression.

"Mom, if you're not going to bed, please come with us. It'll be fun."

"Why are you going to the canyons in the dark and in full make-up?" I ask.

I scan the room, searching for Rona and her pink track suit. But the only pink is the helmet dangling from Thalma's left arm.

"Remember the audition?" she asks.

"Yes. Why are they out there honking if you have an audition?"

"They're going with me. It's a group audition for a beer commercial. They needed night time, don't you remember?"

But Rona . . .

I blink, disoriented. She had been so real! Eithan and Rona, my Tristan and Isolde in their transfiguration, did I dream their story?

"You're freaking me out," Thalma says. "You've got this look in your eyes—"

I raise my hand in the signal I use when I write, when trying to make a mental connection and a fragile cobweb-like thread could be snipped at the hint of a spoken word. Thalma recognizes the signal well and although I'm not writing, she knows enough not to question me.

Me, I'm trying to understand what's happened.

When had I started blurring the boundaries? The airport? Home?

Gila and her two lovers, Daniella's lips, Mike's shaved head, Marina and her lipstick were my mind's creations, but their reality exists. I know it does.

Rona and Eithan exist in many forms, so do the shopping malls, the fashions, the heated political discussions, the crowded sidewalk cafés, and the occasional blasts.

Israel still exists, as far as I know, but Rona hasn't been here at my piano, at my mercy, and she has neither apologized nor picked up where we left off.

I'm so close to tears, there's nothing left to do but laugh as Thalma stares, waiting for an explanation. It was all too convenient to be true, too chocolate-boxy, too impossible. I hadn't even asked Rona, my imaginary friend, how she'd gotten here in the first place. The plot unfolded exactly as I wished, but then frayed at the edges, like me. My need for closure paired with fatigue—and the visit to Israel—took me for a ride on one of my vivid fantasies.

A Small Country about to Vanish

The real Rona may be boring and ordinary, a political clone of everyone else around her. She could be like her friend Daniella, obsessed with plastic surgery, money and her position in society. *She* could be the sex fiend who leaves lipstick marks in dark places.

I'm ready for the truth.

I think of the ad on that torn piece of newsprint—*Piano lessons, all ages, all levels. Call Rona.* I don't need the actual ad as the phone number is engraved onto my memory.

More honking echoes from the alley.

"Earth to Planet Shelli," says my girl.

I smile at her. "Yes, time to land back on Earth."

I'm ready for the risk of reality, even if I discover that I've been a mere blemish on Rona's past, someone who evoked horrible memories. Or worse, no memories at all.

"Please, Mom," Thalma says, "put this helmet on and hop on the bike with me."

"I have to make a phone call," I say. "Good luck, sweetie."

And then, in the middle of my despair, before Thalma can leave, I see a cloud of shocking pink and in it, my Rona.

29

"Hi, Rona," says my airheaded girl. "Mom, I almost forgot. Here's one of my strays. Can we keep her?"

A smile of relief fills my face. "Is she real?"

"You be the judge of that," Rona says.

"Well, get acquainted, you two," Thalma says. "I bought some veggies and stuff, so you've got something to eat. Got to run."

And Thalma is off, leaving me with my fantasy turned reality.

I slice tomatoes, lettuce and onions, preparing an Israeli salad—thinly diced vegetables—with Rona behind me sipping coffee and telling me about her life as if we see each other every day. Her voice in Hebrew feels like never having left home. Quite an idyllic picture, two old friends from Israel meeting in an American kitchen many years later, picking up where they'd left off in the language of their childhood.

I'm happy to have her in my adopted country, but my mind drifts away to a pink dress that followed me across the world and ended up in the jam-packed garage at the bottom of a cardboard box. A faded dress that saw me spend thousands on therapy and alcohol. I have unfinished business—memories to rearrange, nightmares to solve—and since this is my territory, I feel entitled to ask about the painful past. Painful because of her.

I gaze out to the boats and the ocean, sparkling in the sunset. My ocean, my sunset, my kitchen.

Then I say it.

"You treated me like dirt." I sprinkle extra virgin olive oil on top of the lettuce. "You pushed me away as if I'd forced myself on you."

Rona gasps as she had then.

"They walked in on us," she says, her crackly voice pleading with me to understand. "I'd been embarrassed, humiliated, confused."

"*Devastated*, that's what I'd been." I wipe off a tear.

"You're the word expert," Rona says.

I turn to look at her, and for a moment she looks like a fat stranger with slits of lilac-blue in her round face. I want to hurt her as much as she had hurt me.

"It was your home and your room," I say, putting down the olive oil and picking up the balsamic vinegar. "You had certain rights."

"For God's sake." Rona raises her voice. "People were so judgmental in the seventies. You had nothing to lose, with your books and your fantasies and your love of solitude, but I was popular. I had nothing else in my life but being popular. What would you have done in my place?"

"I would have protected you, held you closer. I would have told them to knock next time."

"I see."

"I loved you. I would have been proud."

"Sliha," she says.

"Should I move out of your way?" I ask.

"I meant it as an apology."

Rona smiles. Her violet eyes shine at me and I melt.

"I was a stupid, stupid girl," she says. "Please forgive me."

I let her say the words I crave to hear—craved for years.

"You were always the one, Shelli, but I wanted to belong to the wrong crowd and I was too cool to admit it. I even tried to forget your name. And you were right. We weren't just practicing."

"So how come we were so perfect?" I ask, mollified, because it isn't every day that your fantasy comes true, and in such dazzling colors.

"This is more fuchsia than pink," I say.

Suddenly she stands and stretches her arms.

"Come." She takes the bottle of vinegar out of my hand and pulls me to her again.

30

Rona remembers more. Eva's behavior was surprisingly civilized for a woman of her generation. "I never liked this girl, this Shelli," she had said when she found out the truth. "She'd sit here like she didn't have a home and read and listen to Rona playing. There was always something wrong with her."

Eithan, whom Eva had long ignored, suddenly became her best buddy. She allowed, even encouraged, him to stay the night in Rona's room, as if that would be proof that her daughter was normal.

Eithan was a diamond in the rough and when Rona's life had turned inside out, it was his time to shine. The way he took control was admirable, herding his friends away, telling them to "Scram. Let me deal with this. And, Gidi, you'd better shut your big mouth or your nose will meet my fist again."

No stuttering, Rona had noticed. For the first time, Eithan's speech was flawless, as it would remain from then on.

"I'll ask you once and no more," Eithan said. "You claim that Shelli made you do it, yet your eagerness and your position, the way you . . . Your attitude was that of complete control. Why would you do for a girl what you wouldn't do for me?"

"I was practicing," she repeated, sticking to her story, shocked by his lack of a stutter, his take-charge boldness.

Eithan never asked again or as much as mentioned the incident to her, and for that alone, Rona fell in love with him all over again.

Rona stands in the stylish and functional Californian kitchen, Shelli in her arms, thinking of Eithan and telling Shelli about him, but what she wants has nothing to do with the man she married.

"Let's start you a bath," Rona says.

*

I'm soaking away the long international flight in hot bubbly water. Rona sits on the edge of the bath, washing my hair vigorously, as she had so long ago when it used to be dark.

We have so many stories, so much catching up to do.

"Can I stay with you for a while, until I figure out the rest of my life?" she asks.

"Stay as long as you want," I say, giving in to her touch, so new, so familiar.

"You'll have to fill in the blanks for me," she says, lathering my scalp with vanilla shampoo. "I was too busy restoring my ruined position in the world to notice what happened to you."

I breathe in the aromatic bubbles and think of another scent, harsh and caustic.

The stairwell in Rona's apartment building reeked of chemicals. A long, dark hallway stretched out on each floor, separating four apartments, two on each end of the hallway. The stairwell lights didn't work and during all those years I came to listen to her practicing piano, no one changed the lightbulbs or fixed the shortage. I used to run my hand on the cold and rusted banister, feeling my way up, or down, counting the hallways, counting the floors, counting the stairs with my breath held.

My head used to be so inundated with Ka-Tsetnik that I'd make-believe I was escaping from a gas chamber filled with the killing gas. Each time I'd reached Rona's apartment or the fresh air outside, I felt liberated.

Not that day.

I remember getting entangled in the straps of her pink dress only to realize that it was too tight, too short and that in my distress I'd put it on backwards. I stopped in one of the hallways to turn it around, then I pulled it down, but it barely covered my hips. I could hear a neighbor's door opening on a lower floor and Gidi Ishbitzky or Asher Schwartz saying *lesbos* and laughing loudly at what he'd just seen.

The way down was always long and dark. That terrible day the hallways stretched twice as long, the stairwells were twice as dark, the caustic air a hundred times more toxic than ever before.

This is what Zyklon B did to their lungs, I was thinking as I ran away from Rona's room, from her love and her life. I was crying, coughing, gagging and imagining the gas chambers to have smelled much the same. Imagining their nakedness to have felt the same.

That analogy was a stretch, indeed, but not for me. Not then. I was sixteen, not very popular, and my only friend, whom I'd loved for years, had just betrayed me. Now I have the perspective of thirty-five years and an adult woman's eyes, but then, as I was running toward what felt like the tragic end of my life, I had only the collective memory of my people and a great affinity with those dead six million.

I threw up somewhere on the second floor. That time I felt no relief at all when I got out to the fresh air. I could hear Gidi and Asher, waiting outside for Eithan, still laughing and joking about my disaster.

"Daniella suspected this." "Yes, Le'ora did too." Then one of them said, "Piano fingering each other." And more mean laughter exploded out of them.

I stopped to catch my breath. I waited, hidden behind the night-blooming jasmine—another smell I haven't been able to stand since that day.

Eithan and Rona finally emerged, holding hands, having made up. She was wearing my white shirt and my denim skirt, and her legs were tanned and strong and long. Eithan, without a hint of a stutter, said, "Someone stank up the place. Smells like vomit."

They were walking away into the sunset, literally, holding hands. My clothes were loose on her slimness and she was so beautiful, so loved in spite of what had just happened to us. And I was all alone with it, a pariah who had just had her crotch exposed for the meanest people in high school to see.

I covered my mouth, about to throw up again, then I ran all the way home. There, as I was hoping, I found myself alone. I took the vodka out of the kitchen cabinet and the bottle of aspirin from the medicine drawer. I'd read in the paper about a man who killed himself with that combination.

The pills got stuck in my throat, and I kept washing them down with gulps of vodka straight from the bottle. I put both aspirin and vodka back in their places to cover my actions, went to my room and closed the door behind me for what I believed was the last time.

In bed, still wearing Rona's pink dress, I covered my face with the blanket and finally felt peaceful. I touched between my legs where she had just kissed me and brought my hand, wet with her love, to my mouth. The "Liebestod" played in my head and I, the dying Tristan, imagined that my Isolde would soon find me and choose to sink upon my corpse, transfigured, in verklärung.

In my drugged dream I was trapped in a gas chamber. What I thought were the cries of others was really the buzzing in my ears and the sounds of my own deepening breath. Later I discovered that the deep and fast breathing was a sign that my lungs were getting rid of the acid I'd ingested. I woke in the morning very much alive, but with a terrible stomach ache and a huge question mark concerning the rest of my life.

"So what happened?" Rona asks again, now lathering my clean hair with vanilla conditioner.

I'd never told anyone but my therapist about my attempted suicide. As the truth has remained my secret for so long, I keep it now from Rona, who has enough guilt to deal with, having abandoned her family.

"Well, I ran home, but I hardly remember the rest." I lie as she gives my hair a last rinse. "By the way, what was that smell in your building? The acrid stink in the hallways and stairs?"

"Oh, that," Rona says with a sigh. "My clean-freak mother used to scrub the stairs with a Lysol solution to repel the cockroaches."

"I should have known." I cover up with the towel.

*

A striped beach towel wraps Shelli's skinny body. Her platinum hair cascades down in wet clumps around her shoulders. She seems vulnerable. Her smiling mouth is clean of lipstick and there's one, small vertical line on her upper lip, a line cut by time and sun and smiles. This small line would have sent Daniella screaming to Dr. Miller. Shelli lets it be.

Do Svidaniya. Rona thinks of the woman who leaves behind blood-red lipstick marks. Shelli's clean, natural lips are dry at first, but feel soft and welcoming to her.

Rona has a mental image of the past, of Wagner's music playing, Eithan on her right, his hands inside her bra, and Shelli, supposedly immersed in reading, on her left. Rona had wanted them to trade places, but Eithan wasn't a reader.

Rona lets her clothes fall to join Shelli's towel on the floor. Now, thirty-five years later, she recalls how Shelli could read those horror stories about Auschwitz, flipping the pages with her left hand while her right hand stroked Rona's back. Eithan paid more attention to Rona's front and never noticed. Or had he?

You should see me now, Eithan, loved again. You should hear this music.

*

The creak of the floorboards beneath us weaves within it an echo of another creak, a smaller sound only I can hear: the wheel of my personal history has announced my arrival at the notch of being welcomed into Rona's embrace.

For now I indulge myself, because the glow of her love blinds and deafens me to the future with all its jeers of ridicule, its smells of death, its cries of abandonment, its darkness, its persecution.

I am one with my people. Like them, I have learned nothing.

Rona's hair used to fall forward and get in the way. It doesn't anymore. We're sixteen again in her narrow bed, but no one will walk in on us, no one will interrupt the music this time and kill the composer. An exquisite symphony left unfinished for too long, this time will reach its climax.

*

The End

From the Author
The Middle East flows feverishly in my veins. I now live in Los Angeles, but I was born and raised in Israel and still maintain close ties with family and friends who live and struggle there. I studied fiction writing in the UCLA extension, including the UCLA Writers' Program's Master Sequence with Claire Carmichael. I live with my wife and dog in Redondo Beach, California.

Contact email : victoria@vicavilan.com
Author's website : www.vicavilan.com
Visit Victoria Avilan's author page on facebook

Also by Victoria Avilan: *The Art of Peeling an Orange*

<u>Pro</u>
Interesting backdrop - Middle East

<u>Con</u>
Stilded language. Telling not showing
<u>NOT</u> a page turner.
a young read